Lisa B. Kamps

winning HARD

Chesapeake Blades
Book 1

Lisa B. Kamps

Lisa B. Kamps

DEDICATION

For the women athletes out there, blazing new trails against the odds.

And for the girls who refuse to believe there's no place for them to go!

#FightLikeAGirl

#PlayLikeAGirl

Lisa B. Kamps

Winning Hard
Copyright © 2017 by Elizabeth Belbot Kamps

All rights reserved. Except for use in any review, the reproduction or utilization of this work in whole or in part in any form by any electronic, mechanical or other means, now known or hereafter invented, including xerography, photocopying and recording, or in any information storage or retrieval system, is forbidden without the express written permission of the author.

The Chesapeake Blades™ is a fictional semi-professional ice hockey team, its name and logo created for the sole use of the author and covered under protection of trademark.

All characters in this book have no existence outside the imagination of the author and have no relation to anyone bearing the same name or names, living or dead. This book is a work of fiction and any resemblance to any individual, place, business, or event is purely coincidental.

Cover and logo design by Jay Aheer of Simply Defined Art
http://www.simplydefinedart.com/

All rights reserved.
ISBN: 1979657785
ISBN-13: 978-1979657785

contents

title PAGE iii

copyright vi

dedication v

other titles by this AUTHOR ix

dear READER..xi

prologue 13

chapter ONE.. 19

chapter TWO 29

chapter THREE..37

chapter FOUR 43

chapter FIVE 51

chapter SIX... 65

chapter SEVEN 75

chapter EIGHT.. 87

chapter NINE 97

chapter TEN...102

chapter ELEVEN.. 110

chapter TWELVE... 118

chapter THIRTEEN 127

chapter FOURTEEN..136

chapter FIFTEEN 145

chapter SIXTEEN 153

chapter SEVENTEEN	159
chapter EIGHTEEN	169
chapter NINETEEN	177
chapter TWENTY	184
chapter TWENTY-ONE	192
chapter TWENTY-TWO	200
chapter TWENTY-THREE	206
chapter TWENTY-FOUR	214
chapter TWENTY-FIVE	221
chapter TWENTY-SIX	229
chapter TWENTY-SEVEN	238
chapter TWENTY-EIGHT	246

about the AUTHOR	253
crossing the line PREVIEW	255
playing the game PREVIEW	261

Other titles by this author

THE BALTIMORE BANNERS

Crossing The Line, Book 1
Game Over, Book 2
Blue Ribbon Summer, Book 3
Body Check, Book 4
Break Away, Book 5
Playmaker (A Baltimore Banners Intermission novella)
Delay of Game, Book 6
Shoot Out, Book 7
The Baltimore Banners 1st Period Trilogy (Books 1-3)
The Baltimore Banners 2nd Period Trilogy (Books 4-6)
On Thin Ice, Book 8
Coach's Challenge (A Baltimore Banners Intermission Novella)
One-Timer, Book 9
Face Off, Book 10
Game Misconduct, Book 11
Fighting To Score, Book 12
Matching Penalties, Book 13

THE YORK BOMBERS

Playing The Game, Book 1
Playing To Win, Book 2
Playing For Keeps, Book 3
Playing It Up, Book 4
Playing It Safe, Book 5
Playing For Love, Book 6
Playing His Part, Book 7

Lisa B. Kamps

THE CHESAPEAKE BLADES

Winning Hard, Book 1
Loving Hard, Book 2
Playing Hard, Book 3
Trying Hard, Book 4
Falling Hard, Book 5

FIREHOUSE FOURTEEN

Once Burned, Book 1
Playing With Fire, Book 2
Breaking Protocol, Book 3
Into The Flames, Book 4
Second Alarm, Book 5

STAND-ALONE TITLES

Emeralds and Gold: A Treasury of Irish Short Stories
(anthology)
Finding Dr. Right, Silhouette Special Edition
Time To Heal
Dangerous Passion

Dear Reader:

Welcome to the inaugural season of The Chesapeake Blades!

This new series came about because I needed to do a story about Taylor LeBlanc. You may know her better as Taylor Jennings, the adorable girl with a love of all things hockey from The Baltimore Banners series. You first met her in BREAK AWAY, and saw her again in SHOOT OUT. And, of course, she had a much bigger role in COACH'S CHALLENGE. By the end of that novella, I knew she had to have her own story.

At first, I played around with the idea of making her the love interest for a future Banners player...but that idea didn't *feel* right. Taylor deserved more, and I didn't want her talents out shadowed by another hockey player.

I didn't want to do a rec league series either but, like a lot of women athletes, there really wasn't anywhere else for Taylor to go. Or was there? What if there was a brand-new league, not quite semi-pro, but better than a rec league? Because in this fictional world, there is no NWHL and the rules are a little different.

And so, the Blades were born.

This isn't going to be an easy road for the ladies of the Blades. They'll have to deal with different issues as they learn to come together as a team--from jealousy and juggling two jobs, to dealing with lack of pay and lack of respect, to learning to work with an owner who isn't quite sure what he's gotten himself into and how to deal with it. They'll also be dealing with personal issues along the way, some of which will be hinted at in WINNING HARD.

I hope you enjoy meeting the ladies of The Blades, and that you cry and cheer with them on their journey. And if you're interested in learning more about the NWHL, please check out their website at www.nwhl.zone!

Happy Reading!

LBK

#FightLikeAGirl
#PlayLikeAGirl

prologue

Dreams didn't come with expiration dates. At least, they shouldn't. That was something Taylor LeBlanc had always believed because it was something she had always been told.

What a load of crap.

Reality didn't care about dreams. And—at the ripe, old age of twenty-two—Taylor's dreams were dead.

Done.

Over.

Toes up.

Tagged and bagged.

No matter what kind of spin her dad put on it, she was a wash-up. A has-been. Finished before she started.

Reality sucked.

Big time.

She glanced around the room, at the stripped bed and bare walls and stack of boxes that held the last four years of her life. Fun years. Educational years.

Her glory years.

She blew out a sigh and walked over to the single box that sat on the bare nightstand, alone, holding the last remnants of those glory years. Sealing it seemed so...*final*. Maybe that's why she had saved this one for last—because she knew closing it up and running that strip of heavy clear packing tape over it would be the end.

Not the literal *end*, of course. Her life would go on. She'd leave here, move into her tiny little apartment, get a job. Start something new. Her whole life was ahead of her, right? That's what everyone told her. How this was all about new beginnings. The start of a new adventure.

Except her dream was dead.

"Wow. Drama much, LeBlanc?" She muttered the words under her breath and grabbed the tape gun. This wasn't like her. She knew that. Just like she knew she'd get over it—

Eventually.

She just hadn't expected it to be quite so disappointing.

Heavy footsteps, loud yet hesitant, echoed behind her against the bare floor. Taylor knew without looking who it was—her step-dad. No, her *dad*, period. In every way that counted. Sonny had been there for her from the very beginning. Guiding, teaching. Supporting and encouraging. Telling her to follow her dreams, no matter what.

How could he have known it would all end like this?

"You all set there, Pumpkin?"

Taylor kept her back to him, not wanting him to see the annoying way her eyes were getting all watery. She blinked a few times and forced a smile on her face, hoping that would get rid of the disappointment in her voice. "Yeah. Just need to tape this final box."

Maybe she didn't do a very good job of steadying her voice because Sonny was suddenly standing beside her, one of his beefy hands resting on her shoulder. Solid. Warm. Comforting.

He didn't say anything, just stood there, a wall of silent strength—the way he'd always been. Several minutes went by, long and quiet. Then he reached around her and pulled a black velvet box from the jumble of trophies and plaques that had already been packed. He flipped it open then tilted it up so the overhead light caught on the gold medal nestled amid green satin.

Taylor wanted to yank it from his hand and toss it back in the box but she couldn't—no more than she could hide the tears welling in her eyes. Sonny glanced at her, his mouth thinning for a brief second before he pulled her into one of his giant hugs and patted her on the back with a grunt.

"Why the tears, Pumpkin?"

"I don't know."

"You sure about that?"

Taylor shrugged then rested her head on his broad shoulder, taking comfort in his hold. "Maybe."

He patted her on the back again, maybe just a little too hard, then pulled away and lowered his large frame to the edge of the bare mattress. He patted the spot next to him, the gold medal still in his hand. "Have a seat."

Taylor managed to swallow a groan—barely. She knew he meant well but she wasn't in the mood for one of his pep talks. Not right now. Later, maybe. Right now, she just wanted five minutes to herself so she could wallow in her misery.

But she moved over to the bed anyway and plopped down beside him, trying not to feel like she was nine-years-old again and getting ready to receive a lecture on being a good sport. "What?"

"Why the tears?"

"I don't know."

"Bull—" Sonny cleared his throat, a flash of red tingeing the scar that ran down the side of his face. "Baloney. You're my daughter, I can tell when you're ready to cry. Now what's up?"

How could she tell him without sounding like a whiny little brat who wasn't getting her way? Then again, this was her dad. Sonny LeBlanc. Former head coach of the Baltimore Banners. The same head coach who had led his team to three Stanley Cup championships. If anyone would understand, he would.

Taylor shrugged and ran her hands along the faded denim of her torn jeans. She kept her gaze focused on the torn cuticle of her thumb, searching for the words to explain. Sometimes the easiest words were the simplest, so she took a deep breath and let the words leave in a rush.

"I didn't think it would end this way. I thought there'd be more."

"You didn't think college would end this way?"

"Not college. Hockey. I didn't think the end of one would be the end of the other, you know?"

"What makes you think hockey is ending?"

Taylor looked up, not bothering to hide her frown—or her disbelief. "You're joking, right? It's done. Over. I'm a has-been, Dad."

"You most certainly are not. I don't even want to

hear you say that."

"Why not? It's the truth."

"No, it is *not*. Hockey's in your blood, Pumpkin. You'll always play."

"Not professionally."

Sonny grunted and looked down at the medal in his hand. He snapped the lid closed and tossed it into the box with another grunt then blew out a heavy sigh. "That's not your fault, Pumpkin. You shouldn't beat yourself up over it."

"It's not fair." And yeah, she sounded like a whiny kid who just drew a penalty on the ice. She hated it. But shouldn't she be allowed to be a little whiny? Just for a few minutes? Her dream had died a swift and agonizing death. If there was ever a better time to be whiny, she'd like to know when.

Sonny mumbled something under his breath then reached into his shirt pocket and pulled out a small card. He kept it curled in his large palm, staring down at it like he didn't quite know what to do with it. Then he grunted again and held it out to her.

"I was going to wait until dinner tonight to tell you, but maybe now's a better time."

Taylor glanced down at the scribble on the card without really seeing it. It would take too long to decipher Sonny's writing, anyway. "What's this?"

"There's a league forming. A women's hockey league."

"You mean like a rec league?"

"No, I mean a professional league. Well, mostly. You'd have a contract, get paid. I'm not sure how much." He shifted on the bed then pointed at the card. "It's just four teams to start for now. One of them is back home."

A glimmer of hope took root inside her, pushing away the funk that had been hovering around her for the last week. "You mean a *real* league?"

"Yes. A real league. Tryouts are in two weeks and the season starts in October."

"For real? Like, a *real* league?"

A smile hovered around Sonny's mouth and crinkled the flesh around his warm gray eyes. "Yes. For real. You need to call that number if you want to try-out."

Taylor tried to contain her excitement for all of three seconds, then bounded off the bed and threw her arms around Sonny's broad shoulders. "OhmyGod this is great. I'm so happy. Thank you!"

"Don't thank me, Pumpkin. I'm just passing on the information."

"I'll make you proud, Dad. I swear."

Sonny's arms tightened around her and he pulled her in even closer, his voice thick and gruff when he spoke. "I've always been proud of you, Pumpkin. Don't you know that?"

chapter ONE

Three months later

Winners never quit and quitters never win.

The old adage ran through Charles Dawson's mind, over and over, picking up speed and threatening to split his skull wide open. Would anyone notice?

Considering six sets of eyes were trained on him—yeah, probably.

Not for the first time, he asked himself what the hell he'd gotten into this time. Yes, he was good at marketing. *Damn* good. But he wasn't a miracle worker and he was pretty sure that's what the Chesapeake Blades needed: a miracle worker.

Not just the Blades—the whole damn league. But the league wasn't his problem. Thank God. He was going to have enough of a problem marketing the fledgling team. Let someone else worry about the league, that one wasn't on him.

Not yet, anyway.

And not that it mattered. The two went hand-in-hand, no matter how many times he tried to convince himself otherwise.

Quitters never win.

No, they didn't. But was running for the lifeboats to escape a sinking ship really the same as quitting? Some would say it was simply a question of semantics.

And he wasn't about to split hairs with the group gathered in front of him, watching him like he was their last hope. Like *he* was their lifeboat.

God help them all.

James Murphy, the majority owner of the Chesapeake Blades, glanced down at the colorful presentation folder resting on the shiny desk in front of him. Bushy gray brows pulled low over steely eyes and the thin chest puffed out in importance. Charles knew he was judging the man harshly—Murphy really did have good intentions as far as the team was concerned. Although why in the hell he thought buying into the Blades was a sound investment was anyone's guess.

Money to burn, maybe? A tax write-off? Or maybe the man wanted to be part of something bigger. Hell, maybe he was just living out a childhood fantasy and nurturing dreams of the imagined glitz and glamor of owning a sports team. Charles didn't know and he didn't really care. He didn't deal with dreams and fantasies. He was here to do a job, nothing more.

Damn shame that this job was turning into a major headache that just might signal the end of an otherwise prosperous career.

"Did you have any of the girls in mind, Chuck?"

Charles inwardly winced at the nickname. Christ,

he hated that name. It brought back memories of his awkward childhood, reminding him of those times when he'd been a young bumbling teenager who was a little too round and a little too clumsy to really fit in. A late-bloomer, his mother always said—usually as she was ushering him from one sport or activity to another, anxious for him to find a place to fit in and make friends.

Charles had finally grown out of the baby fat *and* the awkwardness and found his own footing, one that had nothing to do with sports. At least, not the way his mother had hoped.

The irony of his new position as Director of Marketing and Public Relations for the Chesapeake Blades wasn't lost on him. He would have laughed if anyone had told him a year ago that he'd be trying to market a women's hockey team.

A *women's* hockey team. It boggled the mind. But here he was, trying to do the impossible in a market that had a real hockey team—the Baltimore Banners—playing fifteen minutes away. It was doomed for failure before it even started.

But if he could make it successful? Well now, wouldn't that be something? And that's what excited him—the challenge. *That* was why he'd agreed to this job, in spite of the lower salary and its dismal chance of success.

Because sometimes the challenge was everything.

Charles grabbed the last few remaining sheets and placed them in a tidy pile before putting them back in the worn leather bag he always carried. His gaze wandered around the table, knowing the faces looking back at him were still waiting for an answer.

Knowing they were all looking to him for a

miracle.

He hoisted the bag over his shoulder then reached up to straighten the silk tie before turning back to Murphy. "No, I don't have any of the women in mind. I'd like to see them on the ice first. Get a feel for their presence and personality."

"I'd think that reading their bios would have helped with that."

"I didn't read their bios."

Stark silence greeted his announcement, just as he knew it would. Murphy glanced around the table then pinned Charles with his steely gaze, his eyebrows lowering even more. "You haven't read their bios?"

"No. I don't want to be swayed by words on paper. There's too much riding on this."

"I'm sorry, Chuck, but I'm a little confused. And I know I'm not alone. We made sure you had those bios two weeks ago so you could come up with a comprehensive plan. We've already lost valuable time. Do you mean to tell me you don't have any idea of which of the girls you even want to use for this marketing plan of yours?"

"You lost valuable time by bringing in someone who had no idea what they were doing. And while I might be late to the party, I can assure you—I know what I'm doing." Charles shifted the strap against his shoulder then leaned forward, meeting Murphy's stare with an intent one of his own.

"These women can have the most spectacular bio in the world. They could have a list of world cups and trophies and medals and awards by their name. None of it means anything if they don't have that spark and enthusiasm that's going to draw in the crowds you want and need. I don't want the words, James. I want the excitement. The enthusiasm. The spark."

Had he pushed too far? Charles held his breath, waiting for Murphy's reaction. The man wasn't a fool, even if his investment in a women's hockey team was questionable at best. Would he bluster at being questioned? Or would he let Charles do the job he had hired him to do?

Murphy pulled his gaze away and sat back in the leather chair, a thoughtful frown on his face. A tense minute stretched into two, then three and four, before the older man finally nodded. "Fair enough. We brought you in to do the job because you're damn good at it. We'll let you do things your way."

Charles didn't miss the silent *for now* tacked at the end of the sentence. Fair enough, just like Murphy had said. They both had jobs to do, jobs with the same end goal: winning.

"It's my understanding that the team is still downstairs practicing?"

Murphy glanced at his watch then nodded. "For another half hour, yes."

"I'd like to watch, if you don't mind."

"I'm sure that won't be a problem." Murphy pushed out of the chair, signaling an end to the meeting. He clapped his hand around Charles' shoulder then motioned toward the door. "Let's go introduce you to the girls, Chuck."

"James, do yourself a favor—stop calling them *girls*."

"But that's what they are. Every single one of them is young enough to be my granddaughter."

"That may be, but you need to stop. They're *women*. And it's a *women's* hockey team and a *women's* hockey league. I'm going to have a hard enough time getting the market to take them seriously—I don't need you making my job harder."

Charles thought maybe he had gone too far this time because Murphy straightened his lean form and leveled another stare at him. In the end, he said nothing, just clamped his mouth into a thin line and nodded before leading Charles out into the carpeted hallway.

The superficial opulence of the conference room and office came to an abrupt halt as soon as they entered the hallway leading back to the rink. The front office had been designed to impress. To scream *success* and assure visitors—what few there were—that the team was much more than a passing fancy. But it was nothing more than an image, one that disappeared as soon as you pushed through the second set of doors leading to the ice.

The smell of sweat and stagnant water hit him as soon as they pushed through doors. The air was damp and cold, from both the inside temperature and the large sheet of ice encased by the faded boards and scratched sheets of plexiglass. Charles halted, his eyes adjusting to the dim light as childhood memories assaulted him.

He'd played hockey for three years, mostly because his mother had been convinced he needed to play sports. Football, basketball. Soccer. Baseball. He'd done them all. But none of them had been his *thing*, not when he had been more interested in analyzing and studying. In trying to figure out ways to create something better out of something that was already there. In dreaming of ways to make things bigger and better. It was something his mother had never understood, not until his first job out of college.

Maybe not even then.

But out of all the sports he'd been forced to play, hockey held the most memories. The scratch of blades against ice. The burn of muscles rarely used. The rush of wind as he raced for a puck that he was never quite fast enough to get. The smell—God, just the smell was enough to send him hurtling back in time.

He brushed off the memories and followed Murphy along the boards, the leather bag slapping against his hip with each step. Shouts and grunts echoed in the chilled air around them. Two players crashed against the boards with a hollow thud, each fighting for the puck. Charles paused, watching them. The masks of their helmets hid most of their faces, but they couldn't hide the intensity, the *desire*, that burned through them.

It was the same intensity and desire he'd seen on the face of every professional player in every professional game he'd ever watched, no matter what the sport. That had to be a good sign, right?

"Fuck."

One of the girls—no, *women*, he was just as bad as Murphy—muttered the curse as the puck shot free. Both women tore off after it, sweaty ponytails swinging against their backs. Charles bit back a grin then wondered if he'd have to give a lecture on appropriate language before the season started. Hopefully it wouldn't come to that. And if it did…well, then he'd let the coach handle it.

Murphy paused at the end of the bleachers. "Did you want Coach Reynolds to call them over?"

"No, not yet. I just want to watch. Make a few notes." Charles headed to the top of the bleachers then took a seat and grabbed a pen and small notebook from his bag. No decisions would be made today—it was too early. But he wanted this time just to watch. To study. To see if any of the women stood out. To see if any of them had that certain spark, that little bit of magic that would *pop* and make them stand out.

That little extra something that he could build on and use to promote the team.

He knew exactly what he was looking for: charisma. Charm. And yes, even a little bit of sex appeal. It was sexist—he'd be the first to admit it. But physical looks would go a long way in helping to market the team, at least to start. Attractive and athletic, attributes that would entice the market's demographic. Something to hook their initial interest then keep the crowd coming back.

He hoped. A lot of it would depend on the team itself, as a whole, and whether or not they were any good.

He had a few backup plans, just in case. But he could worry about that later. Right now, he needed to get the crowd in the door. This would have been so much easier if he had been called in right from the beginning, instead of joining the front office two months before the season started.

That just made it more of a challenge, and a challenge is what he hungered for. As long as he kept reminding himself of that, he'd be fine.

Maybe.

A shrill whistle split the chilled air, startling him from the hasty notes he was scribbling. The women skated toward the door, removing helmets and juggling sticks as they headed toward the coach. He noticed the sweaty faces, red from exertion, tired but still excited from what they were doing. Would the excitement last, once the season started? God, he hoped so. It would make his job that much easier.

He jotted down a few final notes then flipped to another page and jotted down five different numbers. He tore the sheet from the notebook then made his way down the bleachers over to where Murphy was standing.

The older man glanced down at the small sheet of paper then back at Charles. "What's this?"

"A start. I'd like to see these players once the coach is finished with them."

"We can take care of that now." Murphy grabbed him by the elbow and led him over to the crowd of players huddled around Coach Reynolds. Charles winced when the older man interrupted the coach, saying something to her in a low tone as he pushed the sheet of paper into her hand. The coach frowned, looked down at the paper, then nodded.

"Wiley, Riegler, Woodhouse, Baldwin, and LeBlanc. Mr. Murphy would like to see you. Everyone else, hit the showers."

Five women looked over with varying expressions of curiosity, their voices low and muted as they made their way over to where he and Murphy were standing. Charles casually studied them, his gaze moving from one to the other to the other, analyzing his initial gut reactions to each.

A tall blonde with dimples.

A petite woman with a short mop of black curls and smiling brown eyes.

Another blonde, her platinum-streaked hair pulled back into a ponytail that didn't quite contain the thick waves.

A red-head, with a full pouty mouth and sculpted

brows arched over clear green eyes.

But it was the fifth player that drew his attention. Number 67. Long hair, a mix of light brown and honey blonde, hung down her back, with darker strands clinging to her flushed and damp face. Wide eyes the color of whiskey. A crooked smile that made her look like she knew a secret that you'd pay anything to learn—or that she was up to no good. There was something about her—

"Girls, this is our new PR Director, Chuck Dawson. I want you to pay attention to what he says and help him out." Murphy stepped back then waved his hand, turning things over to him.

Charles stepped forward, his gaze darting back to Number 67. Why was she studying him that way? With her head tilted to the side and those clear amber eyes so intently focused on him? He forced himself to look away, told himself it was nothing more than curiosity, and pasted a smile to his face.

"Actually, you can call me *Charles*, not *Chuck*—"

Number 67 laughed, the sound clear and musical, then stepped forward. For a split-second, Charles thought she was ready to wrap him in a big hug—one he instinctively knew he wouldn't step away from.

And then she spoke and all thoughts of hugs—and every other inappropriate thought that had been swimming around in his muddled brain—vanished.

"OhmyGod, it really *is* you. Chuckie-the-fart!"

chapter TWO

Chuckie-the-fart.

Had she really just called him that?

Taylor glanced around, her face heating as she noticed her teammates' eyes on her. Yeah, she really had called him that. Good Lord, would she ever learn to keep her mouth shut?

It wasn't just her teammates that were watching her, with various expressions of surprise and impatience. Chuckie—or rather, *Charles*—was watching her, too, with startling blue eyes fringed in dark lashes that she didn't remember him having all those years ago. Hell, there were a lot of things she didn't remember him having: his height, which put him at least a good head taller than she was, even in her skates; broad shoulders and a wide chest that filled out his expensive suit. Thick, dark hair that was just a bit too long and made her fingers itch to brush it from where it grazed the top of the crisp collar of his shirt.

A lean, sculpted face and square jaw—which happened to be clenched in impatience right now. His gaze pierced her, annoyance flashing in those deep blue eyes. She started to look away then noticed the way the tips of his ears were turning bright red from embarrassment.

Now *that* she remembered.

"You haven't changed a bit, Chuckie."

The red from his ears traveled across his face, highlighting his sharp cheekbones. A muscle jumped in his jaw and his gaze narrowed even more, making him look like a predator. And God, would she *ever* learn to keep her mouth shut? Because he *had* changed and didn't look at all like the chubby, awkward boy she remembered. He had to know it. How could he not, when he was standing there in front of her looking like every woman's fantasy come to life?

"Tay-Tay. Why am I not surprised to see you here? I guess all your family connections finally paid off, huh?"

Zing.

It was no less than she deserved for egging him on, but the words still hurt—almost as much as the snickers coming from Rachel Woodhouse. Her hand tightened around the stick and she had to fight the urge to run up and cross-check him with it.

Just once.

Hard.

Just like old times.

She glanced over at Mr. Murphy and saw the way he studied her—and not in a good way. The last thing she needed was more trouble, especially not the kind she brought on herself. Yes, the ink on the contract—such as it was—was dry. That didn't mean things were set in stone. Not even close. There were still rumblings that the league might not make it past the first three games. Whether it did or didn't remained to be seen—that didn't mean Taylor wanted to cut her chances short by doing something stupid. She relaxed her grip on the stick and flashed a bright smile at Chuckie.

"So. Chuckie. You were saying?"

Those ocean-blue eyes narrowed on her once more, fixing her with a laser focus that sent a shiver dancing across her skin. Not from cold, though. No, that look was anything but cold. She tore her gaze from his and stared at the toes of her skates, wondering if her face was as red as it felt. It must have been, because Sammie nudged her in the side and muttered under her breath.

"Deets later, LeBlanc."

Taylor nudged her back and shook her head. "No deets to tell."

"Was there something you wanted to ask, Tay-Tay?"

Choked laughter quickly disguised by a cough echoed behind her. Taylor didn't have to look to know the sound came from Rachel. She tightened her grip on the stick and swallowed the urge to elbow the girl in the stomach then forced another bright smile as she met Chuckie's gaze.

"Nope. Just wondering if you were ever going to get around to telling us what you wanted, that's all."

The tip of Chuckie's ears turned red again as the muscle in his cheek jumped. That probably wasn't a good sign and she wondered if maybe she had pushed one too many times. She had to give him credit, though, because he simply blew out a quick breath and scanned each face for a quiet minute before speaking.

"As James said, I'm the new Director of PR and Marketing. It's my job to promote the team and build excitement for this new venture. To sell tickets and get people in the door. I'm going to need your help to do that."

Murmurs buzzed in Taylor's ears, a low drone that set her nerves on edge. She glanced around, saw confusion and curiosity on her teammates' faces, and quickly looked down as she tried to ignore the sinking feeling settling in her gut. She had a feeling she knew what was coming and she didn't want any parts of it.

Shannon Wiley, their primary goalie, pushed to the front. She anchored the helmet against her hip and shook the long strands of blonde hair from her face. Her voice was low and sultry, totally at odds with the razor-sharp bite of her personality that flashed in her deep brown eyes. "You need our help, *how?*"

Chuckie blinked once, a rapid lowering and raising of eyelids framed with thick, dark lashes. Taylor didn't miss the surprise that flashed in his eyes, there and gone before anyone else noticed.

But she did—because she knew Chuckie.

Okay, not really. Not anymore. Maybe not even when they were kids. The man standing in front of them bore little resemblance to the awkward pudgy boy who delighted in tormenting her all those years ago. But she still saw the surprise—probably because she had been looking for it. Taylor doubted that Chuckie was used to being questioned, especially not by a tall, dimpled blonde who looked like sex-on-a-stick but had the quick bite of a striking cobra.

"Part of my marketing plan includes featuring several individual players. All of you, to start with. I want to bring a more personal aspect to the game. To showcase not only the talent but the players behind the talent."

Shannon glanced around then leveled her dark gaze on Chuckie. "So, you want to sex us up? Is that it?"

Chuckie's surprise was clear this time, from the flush of red spreading across his face to the opening and closing of his full mouth. He looked like he wanted to say something but had no idea where to start. It didn't matter because he wouldn't have been able to get a word in, not with the sudden eruption of raised voices shouting questions. Mr. Murphy stepped beside Chuckie and raised his hand.

"Girls, enough. Nobody is sexing anyone up." He turned and fixed Chuckie with a questioning glance. "Isn't that right, Charles?"

"No. I mean, right." Ocean-blue eyes darted to hers and quickly looked away. "No sexing involved."

Heat unfurled low in her belly, the unexpected ribbons of warmth radiating out and prickling her skin. Taylor clenched her jaw and tried to ignore it. No way. Uh-uh. It was her imagination. It had to be. She was *not* going there. No way, no how.

She was still telling herself that when Sammie stepped forward and raised her hand. The voices around them faded and stilled as Mr. Murphy looked at her and smiled. "Yes, Sammie?"

"Mr. Murphy, what exactly does this mean? Because it's not like we have extra time for something like this." Sammie paused and looked around, then turned back to the men. "All of us have other jobs. Some of us have kids. We can't—"

"Charles will be certain to keep your schedules in mind. Isn't that right, Charles?"

"Absolutely." Chuckie nodded but he didn't look quite so certain. In fact, Taylor thought he looked a little surprised and maybe even taken aback.

Did he actually think they were earning a living playing for the Blades? No, he couldn't be that misinformed.

Could he?

Chuckie stepped forward and offered the small group a charming smile. "Flexibility isn't an issue. I'll do everything I can to make this as easy and seamless as possible. For all of us."

More rumblings and murmurs greeted his words. Sure, they sounded reassuring, but Taylor sensed an edge to them, like he wasn't quite certain. Or maybe he was just now starting to realize that the group of women standing in front of him wasn't going to be quite so easily managed as he probably thought.

He opened his mouth again then quickly shut it as a small group of kids entered the rink, laughing and talking as they headed toward the benches. Chuckie's brows lowered in a frown, like he was trying to figure out where the kids had come from and why they were here. Mr. Murphy leaned over and said something to him in a low voice. Surprise flashed across his face as he turned to look at the noisy group.

He must have just learned that this rink—the Banners' old practice rink—didn't belong exclusively to the Blades. Yes, the team owned it. Or rather, Mr. Murphy owned it. But they rented out ice time to local youth hockey teams so they didn't have open access to it. The Blades had to schedule their ice time just like everyone else, for their practices *and* games. Taylor bit back a smile. Poor Chuckie had his work cut out for him.

Mr. Murphy turned back and gave them all a wide smile. "Okay girls, we've taken enough of your time today. Thank you. Charles will be in touch with each of you. For now, go enjoy the rest of this gorgeous weather we're having."

And just like that, they were dismissed. Taylor barely refrained from rolling her eyes and headed toward the locker room, Sammie right beside her. She thought about lengthening her stride and hurrying away but knowing Sammie, she'd just trip her with her stick then sit on her until she got what she wanted.

"Okay LeBlanc, fess up. How do you know the hottie?"

"I don't. Not really."

"I call bullshit."

"Really, I don't. I haven't seen him in…" Taylor paused, frowning as she mentally counted the years. "Wow. It's been about twelve years, I guess. We were on the same team as kids."

"Seriously?"

"Seriously. He was a pain in my ass."

"I could put up with a pain in the ass if he looked like *that*."

"Trust me, he didn't. He was—"

"LeBlanc! A word?"

Taylor cringed and looked over her shoulder, surprised to see Chuckie a few feet behind them, those ocean-blue eyes fixed on her with laser precision. She couldn't read the expression in them but that didn't stop the heat from settling low in her belly.

Sammie laughed, nudged her in the side, then hurried toward the locker room. Taylor ignored her and stood there, watching as Chuckie approached her with the stealth of a predator. Warning bells rang in her head but she didn't move.

"What's up, Chuckie?"

Frustration flashed in his eyes, quickly replaced by something she couldn't quite read. The warning bells rang even louder as he came to a stop in front of her, so close she could smell the faint hint of his spicy cologne.

"Do you think you could manage to stop calling me by that ridiculous name?"

Taylor planted the butt of her stick against the rubber floor and rested her arm along the blade. She gave him a wide smile and shrugged. "I can try. No guarantees. Was that all you wanted?"

His jaw clenched for a brief second, sending the muscle in his cheek jumping once more. He took a deep breath and let it out slowly, then shook his head and smiled.

Taylor nearly stumbled back from the force of that smile, all warm and sexy and too damn gorgeous for his own good. No man should have a smile like that. It was dangerous. It should be illegal.

The smile grew wider as he leaned closer, those startling eyes focused solely on her.

"No, that wasn't it." He tilted his head, his full mouth coming dangerously close to hers as his voice lowered, wrapping around her with a seductive heat that sent tingles of awareness dancing across her flesh.

Taylor wanted to step back, to put distance between them—between herself and that dangerously low, sexy voice. But she couldn't move, not when those deep blue eyes held her in place.

Not even when he spoke again, his words sending tiny thrills shooting through her.

"I have a proposition for you."

chapter
THREE

"No." Taylor clenched her jaw, shook her head, and repeated the word, a little louder this time. "No."

It didn't matter how loud she said it because nobody was paying attention in middle of the chaos that surrounded her.

Her twin nieces—Madelina and Suzanne—were arguing about something. Uncle JP was doing his best to separate them while Aunt Emily chased Tristan, Taylor's rambunctious four-year-old nephew, around the living room with his pants. Tristan had decided a few days ago that he no longer wanted to wear clothes, and keeping him dressed had apparently become a battle ever since then.

Taylor blew the hair from her eyes with a long-suffering sigh and glanced at her own twin sisters, Mia and Cassie. They weren't running around or arguing, but they *were* having a rather loud discussion on the merits of the latest addition to the Banners' training roster. Dad stood in the doorway that separated the huge living room from the dining room, interjecting his own opinions in his booming voice.

Yes, chaos definitely reigned in the house—just another typical Sunday family dinner. Taylor looked around with wide-eyed dismay then glanced at Sonny. "Please tell me I was never like this when I was growing up."

Sonny laughed, the loud sound filled with warm amusement. "You had your moments, Pumpkin. But most of them were on the ice."

Taylor made a low noise—a cross between a grunt and a sigh—then shook her head. She was pretty sure Sonny was exaggerating. Maybe. Then again, maybe not. She'd been an only child for the first eleven years of her life, so maybe she *had* contained her energy to the ice.

A rapid spattering of French erupted from the corner of the room, followed by a loud squeal as Uncle JP caught Tristan and swung him over his shoulder. He grabbed the pants Aunt Emily held out to him then walked toward the sofa and dropped down next to Taylor.

"Your father is right, *ma lutine*. You didn't have to deal with all this, eh? But on the ice was a little different."

"I think you're all exaggerating."

Her mom popped her head around the corner, taking in the chaos with one quick glance, then rolled her eyes before settling her gaze on Taylor. "They're not exaggerating. Dinner's ready."

The twins—both sets—bounded out of the living room, squeezing past Sonny in their hurry to get to the dining room. Emily took a squirming—and now dressed—Tristan from JP and followed the girls. Something that came close to resembling silence settled around the room. Taylor took a deep breath, closed her eyes, and tried to enjoy the momentary respite.

"So tell me why you don't think it's a good idea, Pumpkin."

"Because I don't."

"It makes sense, *ma lutine*. I would try the same if I was in his position."

"But it *doesn't* make sense. He's supposed to market the Blades, not the Banners. And going behind my back to contact both of you was just sneaky. Although I don't know why I'm surprised. I shouldn't have expected anything different from stupid Chuckie-the-fart."

Sonny and JP shared a quick look, one filled with a ton of silent communication she couldn't decipher. Sonny sighed and sat down on her other side, effectively pinning her between the two men. She could sense a battle brewing and folded her arms in front of her, ready to dig in her heels.

"Who is Chuckie-the-fart?"

"The guy who called you. The team's new PR Director. Charles Dawson."

"And you call him Chuckie-the-fart?" Sonny's confusion was clear, both in his voice and in his frown. Taylor blew out another heavy sigh.

"Yeah. Don't you remember him? He used to be on my team when we were kids."

"No, afraid I don't."

"Sure you do. He was a few years older. A little big. He wasn't very good. He used to torment me all the time."

"Sorry, Pumpkin, I don't remember. What I do remember is you always going head-to-head with the bigger kids, thinking you had to prove yourself."

Taylor's mouth dropped open in shock. "I most certainly did not."

Her surprised words were greeted by laughter from both men. She frowned and gave them both a look that clearly conveyed her thoughts. JP leaned over and ruffled her hair, just like he used to do when she was younger.

"Ah, but you did, *ma lutine*. Every chance you got."

She frowned again and waved a hand in dismissal. "Whatever. That doesn't matter anyway. What matters is that he went behind my back and called both of you after I told him I wasn't interested. And you both said yes! I still can't believe it."

The odd sense of betrayal swept over her once more when she thought about it. Chuckie's *proposition* still had her seeing red. He wanted to do some photo shoots and press releases featuring her with her gold medal—and with her dad and uncle. A "family legacy" story, he told her. A real, genuine, human interest piece to draw people in.

He'd had the nerve to tell her the idea had just come to him in the fifteen minutes he'd been talking to the small group of players after Mr. Murphy had introduced him. She didn't believe it. No way.

And then, to make things even worse, he'd opened that stupid, sexy, full mouth of his and said that they had a better chance of drawing in the crowds by using Sonny and JP, that people would take them more seriously since they were real "professional hockey players".

Yeah—because no way could the women on the

Blades be *professional hockey players*.

Anger swept through her once more at the memory of those words. How could he even say such a thing? And how was he going to market the team if that's what he really thought? She should have cross-checked him, right then and there, and knocked him flat on his ass instead of telling him *no* through her clenched teeth and walking away. Maybe then he wouldn't have gone behind her back.

"You need to think about the team, Pumpkin."

Taylor blinked, forcing all thoughts of Chuckie-the-fart from her mind before looking over at Sonny. "I *am* thinking about the team! If he wants to promote the Blades, he should be focusing on them, not you guys."

"I thought he was."

"Okay, so maybe he is. A little. But he also wants to use the two of you. That takes the focus off the team."

"You need to look at it realistically, Pumpkin."

"I am."

"No, you're not. It's a brand-new league and it's going to be an uphill battle to get it off the ground. Anyone worth his salt is going to do whatever he can to promote it and make it a success. Sounds like he's doing just that."

"No. What he's doing is making things more difficult for me."

"More difficult?" Sonny leaned back and studied her with his patented steely gaze. "What do you mean by that?"

"Nothing. Forget I said anything." She tried to push up from the sofa but Sonny stopped her. Great. Her and her big mouth. She shouldn't have said anything.

"What did you mean, Taylor?"

"Nothing. Honest. I'm just tired and stressed a little, that's all. Just ignore me." She held her breath, waiting to see if he'd push, hoping he wouldn't. How could she explain the subtle digs she was getting from a few of her teammates without it sounding like she was whining? So some of the girls were giving her a hard time, saying that the only reason she was on the team was because of Sonny and JP and their connections. So what? It was only a few of them, like Rachel and Jordyn Knott and Amanda Beall. And Taylor knew better, knew it wasn't true. She shouldn't let it get to her—which is exactly what Sonny would tell her if she told him.

He opened his mouth—no doubt to ask her again what she meant—but didn't have a chance to say anything because her mom poked her head into the room and gave all three of them a stern look that was softened by the smile playing around her mouth.

"Are the three of you done? Because we're waiting on you."

"Yup, all done." Taylor pushed up from the sofa and hurried into the dining room, giving her mom a small smile of thanks as she moved past her. She heard Sonny mutter something beneath his breath and noticed the questioning look he tossed her way as he took his seat at the table. She wasn't out of the woods yet but hopefully she'd get a reprieve for the night.

That was all she needed, just a small reprieve. Then she could spend time coming up with a story to give him if—when—he asked again.

chapter
FOUR

The chilled air seeped beneath his jacket, leeching the warmth from his skin. It didn't help that the metal bleacher under him was even colder. Charles ignored the discomfort and tried once more to focus his attention on the opened laptop carefully balanced on his knees. Paperwork was scattered on the bench beside him, the red marks of his hastily scribbled notes muted like dried blood in the dim light of the arena. A cup of coffee, barely lukewarm by now, sat on his other side next to his phone and tablet.

He had an office—if you wanted to call the cubicle that was barely larger than a closet an office. And while the temperature might be a little warmer in the cramped space, he preferred working out here in the rink, at least when the girls were practicing. He had adjusted his own schedule to coincide with theirs, so he could get a better feel for what positives to exploit, searching for little gems he could gather and use to fill his marketing plan. The team only practiced on Tuesday and Thursday nights—as well as Saturday mornings—so if the girls were out here, so was he.

Not *girls*—*women*. Christ, he was as bad as Murphy. God help him if he ever slipped and called them *girls* in any of the press releases he'd been sending out, or in any of the interviews he'd been doing.

Not that the press releases or interviews had been doing much good. Maybe he should slip-up once. Didn't they say that bad publicity was better than no publicity at all?

No. As tempting as that might be, it wouldn't help in the long run. Right now, he wasn't sure anything would help.

He gritted his teeth and kicked the negativity to the back of his mind. He needed to keep looking forward, needed to focus on the positive. It was there, somewhere. He just needed to find it.

Charles glanced at his watch then shifted his gaze to the girls on the ice. A local news crew was scheduled to arrive in the next twenty minutes for a human-interest piece. It was nothing more than fluff, a feel-good filler for tonight's newscast. He hoped it ran longer than the five-second mention on the late-night news another network had run the other day. The station manager had assured him it would but he knew there was no guarantee. If it was a slow news day…maybe.

Charles tapped his finger against the laptop's touchscreen and opened another file, this one an analytics program that measured hits and opens of several paid ads the team was running. Disappointment swamped him and he quickly closed the program. Ticket sales were steady—as in nearly non-existent. No spikes. No hits. No apparent interest. If the Blades—hell, even the league, for that matter—had a bigger advertising budget, things might be a little different. But the budget wasn't there, so his choices were limited.

There had to be something he could do, some small thing he was missing. Something he could capitalize on and exploit.

His gaze darted back to the ice, watching the girls give everything they had during practice. Shouts and grunts echoed back to him, followed by the occasional dull thud of a body hitting the boards, or the clang of the puck hitting the metal frame of the net.

The pipes, he mentally corrected himself.

Wisps of memory rushed through him, transporting him back to that awkward childhood he hated so much. The feel of ankles wobbling in skates that didn't quite fit. Pudgy hands jammed into bulky gloves, the tips of his fingers almost numb from gripping the long stick so hard, afraid he'd accidentally drop it. The groans and taunts of his teammates when he swung the stick at the puck and fell face-first onto the ice.

Way to go, Chuckie.
There he goes again.
You cost us the game, Chuckie.
Can't you do anything right?

He clenched his jaw and forcibly shook the memories off. Playing hockey had never been his thing. Hell, playing sports of any kind had never been his thing. But it hadn't been all bad, not really.

He just needed to really, really concentrate to remember the occasional fun times. And there must have been fun times, because he'd played for three years—longer than any other sport his mother had insisted he try.

And what was he doing, sitting here in the tangled memories of his childhood? He had more important things to do, like getting ready for the news crew. He had chosen Rachel Woodhouse for this interview, hoping the camera would pick up on her blatant sexuality. With her thick, platinum-streaked blonde hair and come-hither blue eyes, along with her lithe build, long legs, and sparkling smile, she should be a natural in front of the camera. She looked like the girl-next-door after the girl-next-door grew up into a sex kitten. Even coming off the ice all sweaty and red-faced and breathing heavy from physical exertion, the camera would love her.

He had originally considered using Shannon Wiley for this piece, knowing she'd immediately attract attention. That idea had flown out the window as soon as she opened her mouth. The woman might look like sex-on-a-stick but she was as lethal as a viper, something he certainly didn't need to come through on camera. For still shots, absolutely. Maybe even some live action footage. The woman was, after all, the team's goalie—and a talented one at that. It wouldn't hurt to showcase some of her acrobatic skills in the net. But actually talking to a news crew? Absolutely not. It wasn't a chance he could afford to take, not if he had any say in the matter.

And then there was Tay-Tay. Christ, he still couldn't believe it. He probably shouldn't be surprised that she was here, not with her connections—and her talent. But here, on the Blades? What were the chances?

Pretty damn good, considering she lived in

Baltimore and her step-dad used to coach the Baltimore Banners. And then there was her uncle, who used to play for the Banners and still worked for the team as one of their analysts. No, he shouldn't be surprised at all. And he had absolutely no problems using her and her family in the team's marketing, not when it would definitely help. His plan was to use her name—to use her *and* her family—to tap into the existing Banners' market. And if he could use that connection to strike a relationship with the Banners' marketing team, maybe pave the way to garner some support, then all the better.

It was just a damn shame that part of him found Taylor compelling and attractive. How was that even possible, when he had been so intimidated by her as a kid? When just looking at her made him feel like that bumbling, awkward, pudgy, inept teenager?

Because part of him was obviously a masochist. That had to be it.

It had absolutely nothing to do with the fact that he might have, quite possibly, had the tiniest crush on her when he was a kid.

A shudder went through him at the morbid memory. Yes, there was definitely a bit of a masochist buried deep inside him somewhere.

He glanced at his watch then shut down the computer and started gathering up the scattered files spread next to him. The news crew would be here any minute—time for him to start doing what he was getting paid to do.

A shout went up, the words "Heads up" echoing around him loud and clear. He turned his head, saw a dark blur hurtling toward him, and tried to duck as he swiped at the object with one hand. His reaction time was too slow and the puck clipped him on the cheekbone, a stinging punch that caused him to pull his breath in with a sharp hiss. He winced as the puck dropped to his side, knocking over the nearly full cup of coffee. Dark liquid sloshed over the files he had just gathered, drenching them and his pants leg.

"Shit." Charles reached for the paperwork, shaking as much of the spilled coffee from them as he could. His cheek burned, a stinging sensation that radiated along the entire right side of his face.

"Shit." He repeated the word, slightly louder this time, knowing he could scream it at the top of his lungs and it wouldn't help. He placed the sopping files to the side then leaned down, his hand closing around the puck resting by his feet. The urge to hurl it back toward the ice was overwhelming but he controlled it—barely.

The control nearly snapped when he saw one of the players come to a stop against the glass, her whiskey-colored eyes wide and glittering with amusement. Had it been an accident? Or had Taylor deliberately shot the puck toward him?

No, it had to have been an accident. Charles knew that if it had been deliberate, his face would hurt a lot more than it did. Even as a young kid, Taylor's shot had contained one hell of a lot of power. It had probably been a loose shot, a fluke. For all he knew, Taylor wasn't even the one responsible for it. He should have been paying better attention.

Or maybe he should have just stayed in his office to work, instead of coming out here.

He climbed to the bottom of the bleachers and stopped near the glass, bouncing the puck in his hand. Once, twice. Once more. Then he looked over at Taylor, his back teeth grinding when he noticed her wide smile and the way that smile danced in those oddly-colored eyes of hers.

She pushed the helmet back on her head and leaned against the boards, so casual and sure of herself. "You okay?"

"Yeah. Fine."

She nodded toward his face, the brightness of her smile dimming for a split-second. "You probably want to get some ice. For your cheek."

"Yeah. Probably." He loosened his grip on the puck then tossed it over the glass. Taylor leaned back and deftly snagged it out of the air, loosely cradling it in her glove as she watched him.

"You're going to have a nice shiner."

"Yeah. Probably."

She nodded then glanced to the far end of the ice. His gaze followed hers, coming to a stop on the man standing there with a heavy camera resting on his shoulder. The camera was pointed in their direction. And shit, was the guy filming?

With the way his luck had been going in the last ten minutes, probably. Great. Just what he needed.

"It's a good look on you."

Charles spun around, surprised at Taylor's words—and even more surprised at the warm smile and slow wink she sent his way. She skated off before he could even close his mouth, leaving him standing there like a slack-jawed kid.

What the hell? Had Taylor been *flirting* with him?

He shook his head, calling himself a fool. What kind of game was she up to? Because there was no doubt in his mind that she was up to something. Was this her way of trying to get out of the photo shoot and interview he had set up with her step-dad and uncle for

Saturday?

Knowing Taylor—yes.

But it wouldn't work. He wasn't that pudgy awkward kid from all those years ago, was no longer content to step to the side and let everyone else take control.

This was his game now. He was the one in charge. And the sooner Taylor LeBlanc realized that, the better things would be.

chapter FIVE

Tension threatened to suffocate him. It knotted the muscles in his shoulders and tightened his lungs, making it hard to breathe.

Maybe, if he was lucky, he really would stop breathing. Just collapse right where he was standing. That would put an end to things. No more headaches. No more struggles. No more drama.

Charles glanced over at James Murphy and squelched a sigh. As much as he might wish for it, passing out would only prolong the inevitable. Might as well just come clean and face the music.

"Things aren't going well, Chuck."

"There's still time."

Murphy's brows jerked up in surprise. His gray eyes focused on Charles, piercing and intent—and filled with obvious disbelief. Charles couldn't blame him.

"Opening night is a month away. Ticket sales are

dismal. Practically nonexistent. We brought you on to help with that but so far, we haven't seen any improvement."

"It's not going to happen overnight, James. We're facing an uphill battle. You know that. It doesn't help that the game coincides with the Banners' first game."

"That's just an excuse. Their game starts at seven. The girls play at one." James looked away, his thin lips pursed in frustration. Charles could relate—he was experiencing his own frustrations.

His gaze darted back to the ice. Practice was officially over but two girls remained: Taylor and Sydney Stevens. They were shooting the puck back and forth, taking shots at the net at the end.

One of the pucks hit the pipes. The noise rang out like a shot, making him jump. Had James noticed? No. The older man was too busy scowling at one of the players.

Damn Taylor. How had she done it? If things had gone according to his plans, she'd be standing on the ice right now, flanked by her step-father and her uncle, posing for the camera and answering questions.

But there were no cameras. No television crew. No reporter.

No Sonny LeBlanc or JP Larocque.

Damn her.

Charles clenched his fists, his gaze narrowing as he watched Taylor race across the ice and take a shot from between her legs. The puck hit the back of the net with a satisfying *whoosh*. Damn shame there was no camera crew to film it.

James released a loud sigh and fixed Charles with another piercing look. "Make it right, Chuck. No more excuses."

Charles watched the older man walk away, knowing that he had just been issued a final warning. Part of him was tempted to just throw his hands up in the air and call it quits. This was a losing battle, had been from the start.

A women's hockey team? Seriously? What had made any of them think they could make a go of this? What had made any of them think that people would even be interested?

And why the hell had he thought he'd be able to successfully promote it?

He hated losing. Hated it with a passion. And making a success of the Chesapeake Blades was nothing more than a losing battle. If he was smart, he'd walk away right now. Cut his losses and move on to something better. Something guaranteed.

Something that paid one hell of a lot better.

But he wasn't a quitter, and he never walked away from a challenge. Not since he was seventeen. He'd be damned if he started now.

He spun on his heel and stormed off to the equipment room with just one thought on his mind: success. At any cost. Taylor thought she could undermine his efforts? Maybe she had, this one time. But not anymore. If she wanted a battle, she just got one.

Taylor was the only player left by the time he returned to the ice. She was focused on lining up a dozen pucks, her back to him when he opened the door to the rink. He took his first step, held his breath as he found his balance, then slammed the door shut and readjusted his grip on the stick. Taylor jumped and spun around, her ponytail whipping behind her. Her gaze caught his and held it for a long minute. Then her eyes widened and a disbelieving smile flashed across her face.

What did she see when she looked at him? Did he look as ridiculous as he felt, wobbling on a pair of old skates while still wearing an expensive suit? He had ditched the jacket and tie and had rolled the sleeves up his forearms but he still felt ridiculous. Over-dressed. Unprepared.

Incompetent.

He clenched his jaw and skated toward Taylor. Slow. Out of practice.

Out of his league.

Screw it. He didn't care how awkward he looked. Didn't care that she was laughing at him. Hell, it wasn't the first time. And he was pretty sure it wouldn't be the last.

"Chuckie-the-fart." She laughed and shook her head then rested her elbow on the butt end of the upright stick. "What do you think you're doing?"

He moved closer, finally finding his center of balance, feeling a small spurt of confidence shoot through him. He pinned her with a steady look, long enough that she finally looked away, the smile fading from her face.

"You think you're so fucking smart, don't you?" The language surprised him as much as it obviously surprised her. Charles didn't care, not when the sudden anger coursed through him, searing him. He moved even closer, not stopping until he was a foot away from Taylor. Her eyes widened in surprise and she slid away from him. Was she afraid? No, not Taylor—she wasn't afraid of anything. But she *was* smart enough to recognize his black mood.

"I'll hand it to you, Tay-Tay. That was a slick

move."

"I don't know what you're talking about."

"Don't you?" He moved forward again, his eyes narrowing. "Why don't I believe that?"

"I don't—"

"You know exactly what you did. Congratulations. You won that round. I never saw it coming. To go behind my back and cancel the interview? How'd you do it?"

"I didn't—"

"Oh, come off it. You did. We both know it." He paused, holding her gaze. "And so does Murphy."

A flicker of unease flashed in her eyes as she looked around. Searching for help? Or trying to figure out the best way to escape?

She pulled her lower lip between her teeth, nibbling the pink flesh for a nervous second before turning back to face him. Charles forced himself to meet her eyes, forced himself to look away from the sight of that full lower lip being nibbled by straight white teeth.

Her shoulders heaved with a deep breath. "I didn't mean—"

"Knock it off. We both know exactly what you meant. Well, congratulations. Murphy's pissed and put me on notice. Is that what you wanted? To totally derail my efforts?"

She laughed, the sound short and bitter. "*Your* efforts? Is that what you call using me?"

"Using you? Is that what you think?"

"It was kind of obvious there, Chuckie. I mean, pulling in my dad and uncle for your little dog-and-pony show? What else would you call it?"

"I call it *doing my job*." The words came out between

clenched teeth. He swallowed back the spurt of anger, tightened his hands on the stick, and leaned closer. "I call it doing everything in my power to promote a team that nobody has heard of. I call it trying to make a go of this team. Of this league."

"Oh please." She laughed again and waved a hand around them. "This whole thing is a joke. You know it. I know it. So stop wasting my time, okay?"

Her words caught him by surprise. Not just the words, but the bitterness in her voice. Charles straightened, watching her for a long minute. A wisp of understanding drifted through his mind, offering him some unwanted insight. He pushed it away. The words *insight* and *understanding* had no place in his vocabulary when it came to dealing with Taylor.

"If you think it's such a joke, why are you here?"

"Where else would I go? Where would any of us go? To some beer league? Because that's all there is."

"Then I'd think you'd want to do whatever you could to make this a success."

"Yeah." She narrowed her eyes and leaned so close he could feel the heat of exertion drifting from her body. "But on our own. You're supposed to promote the *team*. Not exploit me and my family."

"Is that what you're so pissed off about?"

Taylor's jaw clenched, anger flashing in those whiskey-colored eyes. He half-expected her to take a swing at him, or to say something sarcastic and biting in true Taylor-fashion. But she just shook her head and offered him a cold smile. "I'm not wasting my time talking to you. Just leave me alone."

"Or what? You going to beat me up again, Tay-Tay?"

"What are you talking about? I never beat you up."

"The hell you didn't."

She shook her head and tried to skate past him. Charles stepped to the side, blocking her. Her gaze shot to his and he held it, silently daring her to look away. The expression in her eyes was cool. Aloof. But there was something else there, too—just the tiniest bit of doubt.

"I never beat you up."

"Bullshit. You never had patience for me—or anyone else who couldn't play as well as you. And you made damn sure everyone knew it."

"That's not the same—"

"What about that time you boarded me?"

"I never—"

"Yeah, you did. I had the puck. I was trying to take a shot. You got pissed and slammed me against the boards, grabbed the puck, and skated it in."

"I wouldn't have done something like that."

"Yeah? Maybe you should think long and hard because that's exactly what you did. And you scored the winning goal."

"What's wrong with that? We won, right? That's all that matters."

"Is it? Because there was more to it than that to me."

A short, impatient rush of air left her, the sound not quite a laugh. "If you say so, Chuckie."

"I say so."

"So what? I mean, why are you even bringing this up? Why do you even care about something that *might* have happened twelve years ago?"

"Because you're not taking this win away from me, Taylor. Not this time."

"What the hell are you talking about?"

"You heard me. I have a job to do. And I *will* do it—at any cost. Don't get in my way. I'm not that thirteen-year-old kid you enjoyed tormenting and intimidating." And damn, had he said too much? He hadn't meant to tell her that, hadn't meant to admit to any weakness. But there wasn't any gloating in her eyes—just surprise. And maybe even a little regret.

Unless he was imagining that part.

"I, uh, I intimidated you?"

"Christ, Tay-Tay, you intimidated everyone."

"I did?"

"Yeah, you did." And shit, how had they veered so far off the subject? She opened her mouth again, no doubt to defend herself or say something else totally out of line. Charles interrupted her before she could get started.

"It's not happening again. The sooner you realize that, the better off we'll both be. I have a job to do, Taylor, and I'm telling you again, I *will* do it."

"Fine. Then do it. But don't use me or my family. Use the other girls. There's a lot of talent on this team. You should be focusing on that, not my dad or uncle."

"You don't get it, do you? All the talent in the world doesn't mean shit if there's nobody here to see it. I will use whatever I have to in order to get people through those doors. Understood?"

"No. I want no parts of it, Chuckie."

"You don't have a choice."

"The hell I don't." She took a deep breath and looked away. "All my life, I've had people compare me to Dad and Uncle JP. Tell me that the only reason I got anywhere was because of them. Because of my last name. Because of their connections. I'm still hearing it, even now. I don't need you making it worse."

"Making what worse?"

"Nothing. It doesn't matter." She shook her head and tried to move past him again. He blocked her once more.

"You're right, it doesn't. You don't have a choice in this, Tay-Tay, not when Murphy is backing me up on this one."

"That's bullshit."

"Maybe. But that's life. I don't need you fighting me every step."

"I don't—"

"Which is why I have a proposition for you."

Her head whipped around so fast, Charles was surprised she didn't lose her balance and fall. "What are you talking about?"

He would have laughed at the expression of dismay and uncertainty on her face if he wasn't so serious about what he was about to say. Yes, it was ridiculous. Yes, it could seriously backfire on him. Hell, it probably *would* backfire on him. But he was desperate. God help him if she realized how desperate he really was.

"I'll fight you for control." Hell, that wasn't exactly how he meant for the words to come out. It was too late to take them back—although, if he was honest with himself, the blush that seared Taylor's face was worth it.

"Um—" Her mouth snapped shut and she looked around before turning back to him. He ignored the heat rushing through his body at the way her gaze slowly drifted from his skates up to the top of his head. "You want to, uh, fight for control?"

"Not the way you're thinking." Not even close. And damn, now he had to stop thinking of how

Taylor's body would feel pinned under his. "A fight for control of the puck. In the corners."

"You're kidding, right?"

"No, I'm dead serious."

"You don't have a chance in hell."

"Then why are you worried?"

"I never said I was worried."

"Then what's the problem?"

"The problem is, it isn't even a fair fight. You're setting yourself up to lose."

"Am I?"

She moved back and shot a pointed look at his feet. "When's the last time you were even on a pair of skates?"

"Does it matter?"

"Yeah, it does." She looked at him and narrowed her eyes. "I don't want to hurt you."

"Let me worry about that."

Taylor studied him, her sculpted brows pulled low in a deep frown. Silence descended on the rink, broken only by the obnoxious clunking of the aging compressor kicking on somewhere in the back. She finally heaved a heavy sigh and tilted her head to the side, still watching him.

"What's the catch?"

"No catch, because I win either way."

"How do you figure?"

"Like I said, I have Murphy on my side. If you win, you can make yourself feel better and fight me every step of the way. If you lose—"

"Yeah, right."

"If you lose, the fighting stops. No more arguing. No more going behind my back and undermining me."

"Doesn't sound like there's anything in it for me."

"There's not."

"So then why are you even suggesting it?"

"For my own peace of mind."

A smile crept across her face, one that tugged at something deep inside him. He ruthlessly pushed the unwelcome thoughts from his mind.

"You're not very good at propositions, are you?"

"What do you care? You're convinced you're going to win, aren't you?"

"Yeah, but I still lose, no matter what."

"Then you get bragging rights. You can tell all the girls how you beat me up. Again."

She frowned again then finally shook her head and leaned down to pick up one of the pucks. "Yeah, whatever. Okay, fine. But this is stupid. And don't say I didn't warn you."

"Fair enough." He followed her across the ice and watched as she dropped the puck in the corner. "What are you doing?"

"What's it look like? I'm trying to give you a fighting chance. We both know you don't have a shot in hell of catching me if we don't do it here."

"Cocky as always, I see."

"Not cocky—honest." She rested the blade of her stick on the ice then leaned against the boards, looking slightly bored and arrogant. She smiled and nodded toward the puck. "Go ahead. Get it."

"Just like that?"

She laughed, the sound low and throaty. "Just like that…if you think you can, that is."

Charles bit back a smile. He knew exactly how this would play out. As soon as he reached for the puck, Taylor would spring into action and snag it from him before he could do more than blink in surprise.

At least, he knew that's how Taylor thought it would play out. He had something else in mind.

He kept his gaze focused on hers and moved closer, until mere inches separated them. Her body tensed, prepared to launch into action as soon as he reached for the puck. But she underestimated him, her eyes widening in surprise as he pinned her body between his and the boards. Her mouth opened, no doubt to argue or call him names. Charles leaned down and closed his mouth over hers, cutting off any protest she might have made.

It was supposed to be nothing more than a simple kiss. A brief meeting of lips, just long enough to distract her so he could shoot the puck away. He hadn't anticipated the softness of her mouth, hadn't anticipated the heat that flared to life between them. Her mouth opened wider on a sigh—or maybe it was a gasp of surprise. It didn't matter because he took ruthless advantage of it, sweeping his tongue inside to dance with hers. Warm, sweet, tantalizing. He tilted his head and deepened the kiss, his body tightening as she curled one hand along the back of his neck. And shit, he hadn't meant for this to happen, hadn't expected his reaction—or hers.

The sound of a stick clattering to the ice broke through the haze of want and need coursing through him. Her stick, not his. And shit, he needed to stop, needed to pull away.

Needed to remember why he was kissing her in the first place.

He pulled away, swallowing a groan that echoed hers. Taylor's eyes were still closed, her mouth full and damp from his kiss, her chest rising and falling beneath the pads as she struggled to catch her breath. Christ, all he wanted to do was kiss her again. To feel her body pressed against his, to feel her hands tangling in his hair as she came to life under his touch.

He was a fool. Such a fool.

He clenched his jaw and reached for the puck, sent it flying down the ice with an awkward swing of his stick. Taylor's eyes popped open, the heat in their depths quickly turning to frost when she realized what he'd done.

"I win." His voice was shaky, a little too breathless and husky. He watched her, waiting for the biting set-down he so richly deserved.

"Yeah, I guess you do." She took a deep breath then leaned down to pick up the stick she had dropped. Her eyes were hard, her expression unreadable when she looked back at him. "Do you always cheat to get what you want?"

"When it matters? Yeah, I do."

"Then congratulations." Her hand tightened on the stick as her eyes drifted over his body. Could she see how the kiss had affected him? How could she not? Her eyes narrowed then moved back to his. "You got what you wanted. This time."

Charles didn't miss the silent accusation in her voice, or the disappointment. She started to skate past him, her head hung low. He reached for her, anger and self-loathing filling him.

"Taylor—"

She skated to the side, moving away from him when he would have stopped her.

"Taylor, I didn't mean—"

She stopped and looked at him over her shoulder. "Sure you did. Anything to win, right? I can appreciate that."

"Tay-Tay—"

"See you around, Chuckie." She skated away, her head high and her shoulders squared. But he could still see the hurt. See it? Hell, he could *feel* it. And he didn't know what the hell to do about it.

The door slammed closed, the noise echoing around the empty rink. Accusing and somehow final.

And still he stood there, unable to move. Unable to shake the feeling that his little stunt had cost him more than he fully realized.

chapter
SIX

Taylor dug the toe of her skate into the ice and pushed off. The muscles of her legs warmed and stretched, coming alive with each stride. Long, balanced, more natural than breathing.

How long had she been doing this? Years. More than half her life. It was what she wanted to do. What she *needed* to do. It was in her blood—blood that had nothing to do with her step-dad and her uncle. They were related by marriage, not by birth. But nobody cared about that, not when they only focused on her name.

Not when they couldn't look beyond the name and see her talent for what it really was: natural talent. Skills she had worked on, developed and sharpened for as long as she could remember.

Would it be different if she didn't carry Sonny's last name?

Her stride faltered and she lost control of the

puck, sliding sideways as Maddison Sinclair nudged her out of the way. Taylor bit into the mouthpiece and swallowed back a curse as a shrill whistle pierced the chilled air.

Dammit. What had brought that thought on? Where had it even come from? Bitter anger burned low in her gut—anger at herself for even thinking something like that. Sonny was her father, in every way that counted. He had officially adopted her two years after he had married her mom but even if he hadn't, he'd still be her father. He'd done so much for her—for both of them. So why was she having such selfish, immature thoughts now?

Taylor glanced to the side and felt the heat of anger rush to her face. It was *his* fault. Chuckie-the-fart. All of it. If it hadn't been for him, she wouldn't be thinking like this. Damn him and that stupid kiss. If it hadn't been for that stupid kiss—

Oh, who was she kidding? None of this was Chuckie's fault, no matter how much she wished it was. She'd been out of sorts even before that stupid kiss, trying to figure out where she belonged, trying to figure out what she wanted to do.

Trying to face the reality that the Blades were the best she could ever hope for because there was no place else for her to go. For any of them to go. This was it. A lifetime of sweat and hard work. Of broken bones and pulled muscles and cuts and bruises. This was it, the best any of them could hope for.

But that didn't help explain her mood. And it certainly didn't help explain that kiss.

Why had he kissed her? What had he been trying to accomplish? She didn't understand it—or her reaction to it. It was like she'd been slammed into the boards from behind. Like someone had slashed her feet with a stick and sent her flying. Like—

"LeBlanc." Coach Reynolds' voice cut into her thoughts, startling her. Taylor glanced around and noticed that everyone was huddled around the coach—everyone but her.

She ignored Rachel's biting laugh and joined the group. Sammie tossed a questioning glance in her direction but Taylor shook her head, sending her the quick message that she was fine and wasn't going to answer any questions.

Now only if Rachel would wipe that self-serving smirk off her face...

"Just a little over two weeks before our first game, ladies. It'll be here before you know it. Are we ready?"

There was a low chorus of "Yes, Coach", the voices almost subdued. Coach Reynolds frowned and looked around, her dark gaze resting on each face. "I don't think I heard that. I said, are we ready, ladies?"

"Yes, Coach." The answer was loud, all sixteen players answering in unison at the top of their lungs. Coach nodded, a small smile briefly tugging at the corner of her mouth. "That's a little better. We have six practices left—let's make every one count. You ladies have worked hard to get where you are, but we're not done yet. I want to see one hundred and fifty percent out there. Each time. Is that understood?"

"Yes, Coach."

"Good. Are there any questions?"

Rachel pushed her way to the front, a calculating gleam in her eyes. "Do you have the starting lineup ready, Coach?"

"Not yet. I should have that ready by practice on Saturday." Coach paused and looked around, her gaze assessing. "Which means no slacking. From anyone."

Sammie raised her hand, a blush fanning across her cheeks when Rachel and Amanda laughed at her. Coach threw them both a quelling look then turned her attention back to Sammie.

"Reigler. What is it?"

"Have you heard anything about ticket sales? Is anyone but our families even going to show up?"

Coach Reynolds pursed her lips and looked toward the glass. Taylor didn't have to turn around to know she was looking at Mr. Murphy and Chuckie and the other suits that had gathered next to Sonny and JP. The Coach's gaze moved from the group of men and briefly touched on Taylor before moving back to Sammie.

"It's not our job to worry about ticket sales, Reigler. It's our job to get out there and play our best game. Leave the sales to the suits, okay?"

Sammie nodded, a motion echoed by several of the other players. But Taylor heard the undercurrents in the coach's voice. The hesitation, the worry. No, it wasn't their place to worry about the sales, but every single woman here understood the importance of those sales. Without them, there was no team. And if there was no team, there was no place left for them to go.

"Any other questions? No? Okay, hit the showers. I'll see everyone back here Saturday morning, bright and early." Coach Reynolds blew the whistle again, short and low, then nodded toward Taylor. "LeBlanc. A minute."

Oh great, now what? Taylor schooled her face into an expressionless mask. "Yes, Coach?"

"What happened out there? Looked like you lost

your concentration."

"I—" She hesitated, wondering how to answer. It wasn't like she could tell Coach Reynolds the truth. No, that wasn't right. She *could* tell her the truth—she just couldn't tell her *why*. "I did. Sorry. It won't happen again."

"Listen, LeBlanc. I know you're not happy with this whole set-up."

"You do?"

"Yeah." Coach Reynolds smiled, the small gesture brief but understanding. "I get it. I wouldn't be too happy about it if I was in your shoes. But—"

"I know. If it helps the team..." Taylor shrugged and let the words fade into the chilly air.

"That's the spirit. You better get going. I think they're ready for you."

Taylor looked over her shoulder, dread filling her. Yeah, they were ready for her. But was she ready for them?

Not by a long shot. But it wasn't as if she had any choice in the matter.

She skated over to the boards, adjusting her stride as she reached the door. The last thing she needed was to trip and fall. Yeah, wouldn't that look just great. At least nobody was taking pictures or filming anything.

Yet.

She came to a stop next to Sonny, taking comfort in the wide smile that crinkled the corners of his eyes. "You okay, Pumpkin?"

"Yup. Never better."

Sonny leaned closer and lowered his voice. "You know I can tell when you're lying, right?"

"Yeah."

"Then what's wrong?"

"Nothing. I just don't feel—" She stopped midsentence when Mr. Murphy and Chuckie-the-bastard came up to them.

Don't look at him. Don't look at him.

She repeated the phrase to herself a dozen times, not that it did any good. Sure enough, her gaze drifted over to him. Tall, lean, broad. And brooding. Definitely brooding. She could see it in the set of his square jaw, in the defiant tilt of his head.

And in the depths of those stupid ocean blue eyes when he turned and looked at her. Was it her imagination, or were the tips of his ears turning the slightest bit red? Like he was embarrassed or something.

Good. He should be.

And at least she wasn't the only one blushing.

She looked away and forced a smile to her face as Mr. Murphy introduced the small group of people. Taylor barely heard their names, not when she was more focused on the look Sonny was giving her—like he had noticed something between Chuckie and her and was trying to figure it out.

Ridiculous. There was nothing between them.

Nothing except the memory of that stupid kiss that had made her stupid toes curl inside her stupid skates.

She tightened her grip on the stick and flashed a bright smile at nobody in particular. JP nudged her and briefly shook his head. She tamed the smile, wondering if maybe she had gone a bit overboard with it.

A robust brunette stepped to the front, her wavy hair sprayed into submission. Dark lashes, too long and thick to be natural, framed a pair of shrewd hazel eyes. Her full mouth was outlined in a dark mauve.

Professional makeup accented her fair skin and sharp cheekbones, turning her face into some wizard's canvas. The woman looked vaguely familiar. A few seconds went by before Taylor recognized her as a reporter from one of the local stations.

Nerves fluttered in her stomach as she realized just how real things were about to get.

The woman came to a stop and looked up at Taylor. Her head tilted to the side as she studied her, a frown creasing the smooth skin of her forehead. "We have a few minutes before we get started. Would you like to freshen up?"

"Freshen up?"

"Yes. You know. Maybe put some makeup on and fix your hair before we get started?"

"Oh. I, uh—" Taylor swallowed and darted a panicked look at Sonny and JP. They both stared back at her, their expressions annoyingly blank and completely helpless. "I don't, um, I mean—I just had practice and—"

Mr. Murphy stepped forward and placed a hand on the woman's shoulder. "They just came off the ice, Patricia."

"Yes, of course. Well, I suppose we can work with the natural look." The woman didn't look like she wanted to do any such thing. She pursed her lips and looked away, her gaze settling on Sonny then moving to JP. An appreciative smile spread across her face and she moved a little closer to him. Taylor's hand tightened on her stick and she fought against the urge to hit the woman with it.

Chuckie moved next to her and clamped a hand on her shoulder, holding her in place. Taylor tossed him a dirty look. Did he really think she'd do something as stupid as hit the woman?

Yeah, he did.

Of course he did.

"Patricia, why don't we let the men get their skates on while we go over what you wanted to see. Or maybe you'd like to talk to Taylor while we waited? Did you have any questions for her?"

"I think I have everything I need from her bio and stats." Patricia glanced down at the notes in her hand, her mouth moving soundlessly as she read over them. Taylor almost rolled her eyes but Chuckie's hand tightened on her shoulder in warning.

And what was up with that? How did he know what she was getting ready to do?

"Started playing at age six. Gold medal winner. Athletic scholarship. Scholar-Athlete." Patricia kept reading, the words turning into a barely audible mumble. She looked up, a plastic smile on her face. "No, I have everything I need."

Hope flared in Taylor's chest. "So, this isn't like a real interview?"

"No. We'll be doing mostly action shots. The camera will film the three of you on the ice for a little bit as I talk in front of the boards. Then they'll piece everything together back at the studio and run it tonight."

"Oh." The hope flared even brighter. "I can do that."

"I'll need to ask your father and uncle a few things, of course. And Mr. Dawson and Mr. Murphy. But I have everything I need from you."

The hope withered and died, morphing into something else. Not disappointment. No way. It must be anger. Or maybe impatience. Or—

Chuck's fingers squeezed her shoulder once more. "But you will be focusing on the Blades, correct? That was the whole purpose of you coming here today."

"Of course." She waved her hand absently, the smile never leaving her face. "I do know how to do my job, Mr. Dawson. No worries."

Sonny came to a stop next to them, silencing Taylor and Chuckie both. "You ready, Pumpkin?"

She glanced at Chuckie, wondering why the muscle in his jaw was jumping again, then looked back at Sonny. "Ready as always."

"That's my girl." He turned to the reporter, his gray eyes glittering in the overhead lights. "Did you want us to do anything in particular? Taylor has some mean stick handling skills that would be—"

"That's fine. Just whatever you're comfortable with." Patricia smiled and moved toward the glass, coming to a stop next to the big guy balancing a camera on his shoulder. Taylor frowned then turned toward Sonny.

"I think we were just dismissed."

JP approached them, his eyes narrowing as he gazed at Chuckie's hand where it still rested on her shoulder. She felt Chuckie stiffen a split second before he dropped his hand, then smothered a laugh when JP's gaze cleared. Yeah, right. His concern was seriously misplaced if he thought there was anything going on between them.

"Don't worry about her, *ma lutine*. We have more important things to do, eh?"

"Yeah. I guess." She twirled the stick in her hand then followed Sonny and JP out to the ice. She felt a hand drop to her shoulder once more and turned around, surprised to see the serious expression on

Chuckie's face as he stood behind her.

"I really need you to go out and wow them, Tay-Tay."

She glanced down at his broad hand. "Yeah. Sure. No problem." She quickly shrugged his hand from her shoulder and stepped onto the ice, forcing all thoughts of deep blue eyes and a warm, toe-curling kiss from her mind.

chapter
SEVEN

These girls have a long road ahead of them and quite frankly, in this reporter's opinion, I don't see much chance for them.

Taylor swallowed back the fury bubbling through her veins and replayed the clip. It was two minutes long. Two full minutes, filled with the same condescending, negative tripe as the bitch's last line.

A clip of Taylor stumbling on the ice at the end of practice.

I don't see much chance for them.

A clip of them huddled around the coach, their weak "Yes Coach" sounding weary and unenthusiastic.

I don't see much chance for them.

Another clip. This one of Chuckie talking to her, his hand on her shoulder, right before she went back onto the ice. The look on her face spoke volumes: anger, resignation, frustration. Is that how she always looked? No, it couldn't be. No way.

Oh God, it was awful. Worse than awful. The bits and pieces about Dad and Uncle JP and the Banners were great, bubbling over with enthusiasm. But the blips about the Blades—about *her*—were horrifying.

Depressing.

I don't see much chance for them.

She was going to kill Chuckie. Literally.

The screen on her phone lit up, flashing another number, one she didn't recognize. She flipped the phone upside down and ignored it, just like she'd been doing for the past hour, ever since the piece had aired.

This was bad. This was worse than bad.

And as much as she wanted to blame Chuckie, to lay all of this at his feet, she couldn't. Even she knew he wouldn't have done this deliberately. He couldn't have known how bad it was going to be. Could he?

No, he couldn't. It was his job to promote the team, not knock it down. There was no way he could have known.

That didn't mean she didn't want to kill him.

She hit replay and watched the clip again, searching for anything the least bit positive in it. The search was an exercise in futility because nothing positive existed. She should just turn it off. Pretend it never happened.

Go to sleep and wake up for work tomorrow and hope the whole thing would just disappear. It was just a stupid news clip, right? How many people actually watched the news until the end? Hardly anyone, right?

Taylor could almost believe that, if her phone hadn't started blowing up with calls right after the piece aired.

I don't see much chance for them.

"Screw you." Taylor leaned forward and grabbed

the glass of iced tea as she hit replay once more. The sound of the doorbell startled her, causing her to spill some of the tea down the front of her shirt. She stared down at the brownish streak spreading across her shirt and sighed.

The doorbell buzzed again, louder this time. Taylor didn't want to answer it—she wasn't expecting anyone and figured if she ignored it, whoever it was would just go away.

She swore under her breath when the doorbell buzzed a third time then pushed herself off the sofa. Maybe it was just one of the kids who lived in the building, trying to sell something. Chocolate bars, maybe. She could go for some chocolate right now.

Except it wasn't a kid standing at the door.

Taylor blinked, her mouth dropping open in shock when a pair of deep ocean blue eyes stared back at her. She snapped her mouth closed and tightened her hand on the knob, ready to slam the door in Chuckie's face. He must have sensed what she was about to do because he stepped inside, his hand reaching out to hold the door open.

"I'm sorry."

"Go to hell." Taylor tried closing the door but he wedged his body against it, stopping her. "I mean it, Chuckie. Get out."

"I'm sorry. I didn't know—"

"Yeah, right."

"I swear it, Taylor. I had no idea."

She studied him for a long second, sensing the honesty in his words. And it didn't take a master of observation to see the misery in his eyes—the same misery that had been swamping her since the piece had run.

He looked tired. Worn out. Dark stubble covered his jaw and his hair was tousled and messy, like he'd been running his hands through it for the past hour. Faded jeans clung to his lean hips. The sleeves of the old, stretched out sweatshirt were pushed up past his elbows, exposing muscled forearms covered in the barest dusting of dark hair. She tried to hide her surprise when her gaze skimmed over the college insignia embroidered on the chest of the sweatshirt.

The man in front of her didn't look like the Chuckie she remembered—not the awkward boy from her childhood, and not the crisp, suit-clad man from the last few weeks. The man in front of her looked completely different. Tired. Stressed. Dejected.

Miserable.

Taylor sighed and loosened her hold on the door. She didn't step back, though, or invite him in. "What do you want, Chuckie?"

"I came to say I'm sorry." He held up a cardboard six-pack of a local craft brew. "And to commiserate."

"Chuckie, I don't think—"

"Misery loves company, right? Besides, this is probably the last time I'll see you. I'm pretty sure I'm going to be out of a job tomorrow."

Taylor hesitated, questioning the wisdom of what she was about to do. Then she sighed and stepped back. Chuckie gave her a half-hearted smile and moved past her, his gaze sweeping the small apartment.

She held her breath, waiting for him to comment. To say it was smaller than he expected; to ask why it wasn't fancier or more glamorous. It wouldn't be the first time she had been asked those questions. For some reason, people automatically assumed she had money to burn because of her family. Or that her family took care of her and paid her bills.

"Nice place. Cozy."

"Yeah. Cozy." Taylor shut the door and looked around. The overstuffed loveseat, upholstered in a striped peaches-cream motif, sat across from the flat screen television mounted on the wall. The single remote and a large glass vase filled with potpourri sat on the old wooden trunk that served as a coffee table. A refinished desk sat against the far wall, its surface cluttered with her laptop and scattered paperwork.

The dining alcove was just beyond the living room, adjacent to the small kitchen. A short hallway led back to the bathroom and small bedroom. The apartment was small and efficient, which was all she needed.

And probably all she would be able to afford for the next five or ten years.

Chuckie lowered himself to the loveseat and placed the six-pack on the old trunk. He hesitated, a frown crossing his face when he noticed the news clip playing on the television. The frown turned into a scowl when he looked at her.

"Would you mind turning that off? I can't stand watching it again."

Taylor grunted her agreement then grabbed the remote and powered everything off. Silence settled over the room, awkward and stifling.

So now what? Should she offer him something to drink? Probably not, since he was busy opening a bottle of beer. She ran her hands along the sweatpants and looked around, unsure of what to do now.

Chuckie offered her the opened bottle of beer. She stared at it, not moving.

"It's not going to bite Tay-Tay."

"I know that." She stepped forward and took the bottle from him, then glanced around as she tried to figure out where to sit. The loveseat was too small, too crowded with Chuckie sitting there. But it wasn't like she had much choice, not unless she grabbed one of the chairs from the dining room and dragged it over.

She bit back a sigh and finally sat down, scooting as close to the side of the loveseat as she could. That only left a few inches separating them.

Chuckie shot her a questioning glance then reached for another beer, uncapping it and raising it in mock salute. "To careers cut short."

"Um—"

He took a long swallow, sighed, then leaned his head against the back of the loveseat and closed his eyes. "Christ. What a colossal fuck up."

"I'll drink to that."

He grunted but said nothing, just sat there with his head tilted back and his eyes closed. Taylor watched him, her eyes drifting over his broad shoulders and chest and down to his jean-clad legs. She forced herself to look away, telling herself to ignore the heat flaring in her stomach.

Her eyes darted back to Chuckie once more, studying the hand carelessly resting against his thigh. The long fingers curled slightly toward his palm, the nails short and clean. He had nice hands. Not smooth, but not heavily callused or torn up. Large. Strong.

And oh God, why was she staring at his hands? This was Chuckie. *Chuckie-the-fart.* She had no business looking at his hands, even if she did have a weakness for them.

She forced her gaze away once more and took another sip of beer. Silence stretched around them, not quite uncomfortable but not exactly companionable, either. Taylor searched her mind, trying to think of something to say.

Wondering if she should ask him again why he was here.

"I really am sorry, Tay-Tay."

"Yeah, well." She sighed and shook her head. "Shit happens. Nothing we can do now."

He turned his head to the side and cracked open one eye. "Why do I have the feeling you're holding back?"

Taylor shrugged and leaned forward, putting the bottle on the coffee table.

"Well, whatever the reason, thank you." He closed his eye and sighed. "Tomorrow is going to suck."

"You really think you're going to get fired?"

"Yup."

"It wasn't exactly your fault."

"I'm the one who set it up."

"Yeah, but it's not like you had any control over what came out of the bitch's mouth."

Chuckie opened his eyes again and looked over at her, a small smile tugging at the corners of his mouth. "Better be careful, Tay-Tay. It almost sounds like you're defending me."

"No. I just—" Her mouth snapped closed and she looked away. She *was* defending him. And the worst part was, she meant it. Yes, she might want to blame everything on Chuckie, but what she said was true: he couldn't control what came out of anyone's mouth.

"You just, what?"

"Nothing." She reached for the beer and took a long swallow, using the few seconds to regroup her thoughts. "If it makes you feel any better, I'll be catching shit on Saturday at practice."

"Why would you catch shit? You didn't do anything wrong."

"Won't matter. A few of the players will blame it on me. They, uh, they don't exactly like me."

"Why not?"

"I told you. A few of them think the only reason I'm on the team is because of Dad. That's why I didn't want to do it. The interview, I mean."

Chuckie was quiet for a long minute, his gaze too intense, seeing too much. She forced herself to look away, prayed that her face wasn't stained bright red.

Another long minute stretched around them, finally broken by the sound of a heavy sigh. Chuckie's hand brushed against her shoulder. The tips of his fingers grazed the sensitive flesh of her neck then dropped away.

Taylor didn't move. She couldn't move, not when his touch had frozen her in place. But how could she be frozen, when her skin was suddenly burning from his touch? It didn't make sense.

"I should have listened to you."

She blinked, forced her head to move. Chuckie was watching her, those deep blue eyes focused on her with an intensity that sent shivers dancing across her skin. "Huh?"

"I said I should have listened to you. I'd say next time I will, but I don't think there's going to be a next time."

"So you're really positive you're going to get fired?"

"Hell, I'd fire me. Don't see why Murph would do any different."

Taylor stared down at the bottle, her mood sliding

downhill at Chuckie's certainty. Why did the thought of never seeing him again sadden her? It wasn't like they knew each other. They didn't even really like each other that much.

Or maybe it wasn't really Chuckie's fatalist mood that was depressing her. Maybe it was the sudden certainty that all of her dreams were about to disappear. The reporter's words came back to her, taunting.

I don't see much chance for them.

Is that what everyone thought? If it was, maybe the whispered rumors of the league not lasting past three games had some basis in fact. And if that was the case—

Taylor sighed and took another sip of beer, longer this time. She wiped her mouth with the back of her hand then dropped her own head against the loveseat cushion. "This sucks."

"Yup. Pretty much."

"This whole thing was never going to work out, was it?"

She sensed rather than saw Chuckie straighten. "What thing? What are you talking about?"

"The whole league—if you can call it that. It was just one big joke, wasn't it? Over before it finished."

"The league isn't over, Taylor."

"Yeah it is. I'm not stupid. None of us are. If there aren't any ticket sales, there's no money coming in. And if there's no money, there's no team. Doesn't take a genius to figure that out."

"The team isn't going anywhere."

She turned her head to the side and opened her eyes. Chuckie was close—too close. And those eyes of his were fixed on hers, watching her, holding her in place. Her breath caught in her lungs and she forced her eyes closed.

"Yeah it is. We both know it."

"Sounds like you're quitting before you even get started."

"Isn't that why you're doing, Mr. I-know-I'm-getting-fired-tomorrow?"

"I'm good at what I do, I can find another job on Monday. And that's all it is: a job. But you—Taylor, you've always been destined for more. Hockey is your whole life. That's all you've ever dreamed about. Don't give up on your dreams, Tay-Tay."

Her eyes popped open, surprise filling her at the conviction of his words—and at how close he had come to the truth. "What makes you so sure of that?"

Something flashed in his eyes, a spark or a reflection that caused heat to flare inside her once more. Then he blinked and it was gone, making her wonder if she had imagined it.

He leaned back, putting some distance between them, then offered her a crooked smile, one that made him look dangerously boyish and charming. "I may have had a crush on you when were kids."

"What?" She sat up, nearly bumping her forehead against his nose. Beer splashed out of the bottle, landing on her sweatpants. She ignored it, too stunned to do anything but stare at him in open-mouthed shock.

He chuckled, the sound warm and low, and reached out with one finger to close her mouth. "Why do you look so surprised?"

"Because—because—" She swallowed and took a deep breath. "We were *kids*. I was, like, ten. And you—you were—"

"The slow, fat kid."

"No! That's not what I going to say!"

"Why not? It's the truth."

Taylor ignored him, not knowing how to reply to that. She shook her head. "You were *thirteen*. That's just gross."

"Gross?" He sat back, his brows lowering in a deep frown. "Thanks for that ego-boost, Tay-Tay. Just what I needed."

"I didn't say *you* were gross. Just—ohmyGod, I was *ten*."

"And now you're not. Still grossed out?"

She opened her mouth then promptly shut it again. What was he saying? Or was she merely reading too much into things? Because certainly he couldn't mean he still had a crush on her.

Could he?

He leaned closer, the heat in his eyes burning her. But it was a slow burn, one that started deep in her belly. A burn that promised so much more. His voice when he spoke was low, filled with the same promise reflected in his eyes.

"Nothing to say?"

Taylor shook her head, knowing that anything she said would come out as a small squeak—if she could even manage to get any words out. That dangerously charming grin curled the corners of his mouth again. He reached for the bottle in her hands and eased it from her numb fingers, his eyes still focused on her as he placed the bottle on the table.

Then he moved even closer, mere inches separating them. Taylor didn't miss the silent question in his eyes, the uncertainty that flashed in their depths. She reached up, her trembling fingers grazing the soft stubble outlining his jaw.

And then his mouth was on hers. Soft, warm. Hesitant and seeking. Taylor sighed and leaned into the kiss, giving herself over to the sensations crashing against her.

chapter
EIGHT

All Charles wanted was a kiss. Just one kiss, just to see if it was as sweet as the kiss he had stolen last week.

But this—this was anything but sweet.

Taylor sighed and leaned into him, her arms draping behind his neck. And God, just that much nearly sent him over the edge. Her mouth opened under his and his tongue swept in, dancing with hers. Hot. Wet.

Teasing.

Tormenting.

He tightened his arms around her, pulling her closer, all lean muscle and small, firm, curves. Her fingers drifted into his hair, grazed the sensitive skin along the back of his neck then slowly traced the curve of his shoulders and arms before moving back up. Over and over, her tentative touch driving him as wild as the slick thrusting of her tongue against his.

Had he really thought one kiss would be enough?

He'd been a fool.

He shifted on the small loveseat, tugging her pliant body until she straddled him. Her hips rocked against the length of his erection, hesitated, rocked again. And shit, any more of that and he really would go over the edge.

He pulled his mouth from hers and kissed the side of her neck, nibbled the flesh just under her ear. Short nails dug into his shoulders as she sighed and tilted her head back, exposing the long column of her throat. Charles took immediate advantage and ran his mouth along her tender skin, pausing to kiss the spot where her pulse beat wildly.

He cupped the back of her head, his fingers tugging at the elastic band that held her hair back. The long strands fell free, cascading down her back in a waterfall of molasses and honey, and curled around his hands. Soft as silk, thick and smooth and somehow alive.

He tilted her head forward and leaned up, capturing her full mouth once more.

Sweet? There was nothing sweet about Taylor. There never had been. Why had he thought her kiss would be sweet?

Why had he thought he could stop with just a kiss?

He ran his hands along her sides, captured the hem of the soft t-shirt, and dragged it up, his touch light and teasing against flushed skin. She pulled back, her glazed eyes focused on his as she grabbed the shirt and pulled it over her head. Her hair drifted around her shoulders, the ends swinging against the hardened nipples of her firm breasts.

He reached out, surprised to see his fingers trembling as he grazed one nipple with the back of his hand. Taylor's breath left in a rush as her head tilted back once more. Her back arched, the action pushing those small, firm breasts even closer.

Charles wrapped his hands around her waist and pulled her closer, his mouth closing over the tight peak of a dusky nipple. Taylor sighed, the sound short and breathy. Her hips rocked against his once more as her hands curled around the back of his head and held him in place.

He pulled the nipple deeper into his mouth, sucking, twirling his tongue around the hard peak before nipping it with his teeth. A shudder went through her, followed by a long moan.

He pulled his mouth away and looked up at her. The soft light from the single lamp on the end table fell over her, casting her body in a warm glow. The faintest of blushes colored her cheeks. Her lips were full and wet from his kisses.

His kisses.

Something primitive stole over him. Not just desire. No, this was much more. The need to possess, to mark her as his own. Charles shook his head and nearly laughed at the notion.

Taylor was her own woman. There wasn't a man alive who could possess her.

Not even him.

And God help whoever tried.

The knowledge didn't lessen the desire, the need. Temporary insanity, it must be. He'd never experienced this need to possess before—insanity had to be the only explanation.

Her lids fluttered open. Eyes the color of whiskey drifted to his, watching him. Their depths glowed with glazed passion, with desire. With need.

With uncertainty.

Charles tightened his hands on her waist, felt her long legs tighten around his in response. He cleared his throat and forced himself to ask the question he didn't want to ask.

"Do you want me to stop?"

Her tongue darted out and swiped across her lower lip, the action tightening something in his gut. He held his breath then let it out in a rush when she shook her head.

"No." She shook her head again, her gaze darkening as she watched him. "No. I don't want you to stop."

Charles reached for her, pulling her even closer as he claimed her mouth. This kiss was different—deeper, harder. Possessing. But it still wasn't enough. Not nearly enough.

He wanted *her*. All of her. To feel her. Touch her. Taste her. Every inch. Every curve and dip.

He reached between them and grabbed the hem of his sweatshirt, shifting as he tried to pull it off. Their hands tangled together and Taylor pulled back, a soft smile curling that luscious mouth. She batted his hands away and took control of the shirt, peeling it over his head and tossing it to the floor.

Her gaze drifted over his body, hunger flaring in her eyes as she traced the lines of his shoulders and chest with her hands. "You've filled out, Chuckie."

He laughed and palmed one of her breasts, rolling the nipple between his thumb and forefinger. "So have you."

A shadow crossed her eyes and she shook her head, pulling back a little. Her arms moved, like she wanted to cover herself. "Not really."

He caught one arm, pulling it away when she would have crossed it in front of her chest. "Yes. You have. You're perfect."

Her arm relaxed under his touch and her lips parted in surprise. Why would she be surprised? She *was* perfect, small and firm, with beautiful dusky nipples that hardened even more under his gaze.

He lowered his head and pulled one into his mouth again, groaning at her sharp sigh as she rocked against him. Her hands tightened on his arms, her fingers kneading the muscles of his biceps as he licked and sucked. She whispered his name, the sound nothing more than a soft sigh.

"Chuckie."

He stilled, gently eased the nipple from his mouth, and tilted his head back. Taylor's lids fluttered open and she stared down at him, confusion glittering in the warm depths of her eyes.

"What?"

"Do me a favor: don't call me *Chuckie*."

"But it's your name."

"No, it's not. It's *Charles*. I'll even accept *Chuck* in a pinch. But for God's sake, don't call me *Chuckie*. Especially not right now. You're making me feel like that awkward little boy again."

She laughed, the sound low and throaty and totally dangerous. One hand drifted to the center of his chest, her fingers twirling in the light dusting of dark hair as her hips rocked against the rigid length of his straining erection. Once. Twice. Once more.

"You're definitely not a little boy." She leaned forward and caught his lower lip between her teeth, playfully nipping before sitting back. "*Chuckie*."

He growled—there was no other word for it—and

pulled her closer, his arms tightening around her waist. Then he pushed to his feet, almost laughing when a small squeak of surprise escaped her. She wrapped her arms around his neck and held on.

"What are you doing?"

"Carrying you to the bedroom." He sensed her hesitation and halted in the middle of the hallway, looking down at her. "Is that okay?"

"Um, my room's a bit messy."

"Can you reach the bed?"

"Yeah, but—"

"Then that's all I care about." He caught her mouth with his, silencing whatever protest she had been ready to utter. She wrapped her legs high around his waist and kissed him back, her soft little murmurs driving him wild as he made his way down the hall.

And then they were in her room. She dropped her legs, her body sliding against his. Her hands closed around his shoulders and tugged. She fell back onto the mattress, taking him with her.

Charles claimed her mouth again, his hand reaching between them and tugging at the loose sweatpants she wore. Her hips rocked and shifted as he worked the material down her legs, not stopping until she was bared to his sight.

The breath caught in his chest as he stared down at her, drowning in the sight of her body. Small, firm breasts. Lean waist. The gentle flare of hips. Well-defined thighs and tight, shapely calves. The body of an athlete, complete with the faint scars and bruising of battles won and lost.

He swallowed and looked up, noticed her watching him. He knelt next to her, his hand drifting along the lines and curves of tight, firm flesh. "You're beautiful, Taylor."

Her body relaxed, as if she had been waiting to hear criticism instead of praise. A small smile teased her lips as she reached for him, her fingers tracing the thin line that disappeared into the waistband of his jeans.

"Your turn."

He sucked in a deep breath when her hand cupped his erection beneath the denim. He reached down, folded his hand over hers, and pressed himself against her palm. His cock strained against the zipper, eager for release.

Eager for more of her touch.

Her fingers fumbled for the button, popped it open and reached for the zipper, easing it down. She rolled to her knees and pushed the denim past his hips, reaching between them to curl her fingers around the rigid length of his cock when it sprung free.

Charles clenched his jaw, his head falling back. Christ, her touch felt so good. Liquid fire, burning him. Searing him. He ached, every inch of him throbbing in sweet agony as she stroked him. Hard. Fast. His hips thrust in time to the rhythm of her hand, seeking the release her touch promised.

Not yet. Not like this.

He reached between them and closed his hand over hers, slowing her touch until he was safely away from the edge.

For now.

He leaned forward and captured her mouth, reaching into his back pocket with his free hand. He snagged his wallet and opened it, his fingers searching for the condom. He tossed the small package on the mattress next to him then threw the wallet to the side.

It bounced off the bed and hit the floor with a hollow thud.

Taylor leaned closer, the firm roundness of her breasts pressed flat against his chest. His heart beat faster, a steady thud under his ribs. Could she feel it? She must, just as he felt the steady beat of her own heart.

He pulled her closer and deepened the kiss, drinking in each little sigh and moan that escaped her.

Sweet?

How had he ever made the mistake of thinking anything about this woman was sweet? Taylor was fire and spice, heady and intoxicating. So much more than anything his immature and ignorant fantasies had been able to conjure all those years ago.

More than anything he had fantasized about weeks ago, when he had first seen her on the ice.

He ran his hand along her arm, down across the gentle flare of her hip, then dipped his fingers between her legs. She arched against him, her fingers biting into the flesh of his shoulders when he grazed her clit with his knuckle. And fuck, she was already wet. So wet. So hot.

She spread her legs, her hips arching against his touch when he slid one finger inside her. He broke the kiss, dragged his mouth down along her throat, then shifted until she fell to her back. He straddled her, kissing every inch of her flushed skin until he reached the hot flesh he was searching for.

He grabbed one of her legs and draped it over his shoulder, then bent his head and ran his tongue along her clit. Her hands threaded in his hair, her grip tight on his head as her hips rocked under every kiss, every lick, every nibble.

Her breathing came faster, her chest rising and falling with each harsh gasp as her body arched under his touch. He slid two fingers inside her, in and out. Faster. Harder. Her muscles tightened and clenched around him as he stroked her clit with his tongue. He raised his eyes, watching as her head moved from side to side, the soft strands of her long hair tangling around her. And then her body tightened, her back arching for one long second before she shattered.

Charles swallowed back his own groan and reached for the condom, sheathing himself with it as he kicked off his pants. Then he was braced on top of her, her long legs wrapping around his waist as he plunged into her.

Filling her. Stretching her.

And God, she was tight. So fucking tight. Hot. Wet.

He grabbed her hips and held her still, driving into her with a frenzied need that scared him. She reached for him, his name falling from her lips in a ragged whisper of need. He dipped his head and claimed her mouth, their tongues mating in a rhythm as wild and frenzied as their bodies.

She stiffened under him once more, a moment frozen in time before her body shattered beneath him. It was too much, he couldn't hold back, not with the way she felt.

With the way he felt inside her.

Charles clenched his jaw and drove into her. Hard. Deep.

Once.

Twice.

His body stilled, every muscle pulled taut as his own climax washed over him, over and over, the intensity of it searing something deep inside him. He sucked in a deep breath, trying to fill his lungs with air, then collapsed on top of Taylor as stars flashed behind his lids.

Seconds went by, or maybe minutes. Hell, it could have been an hour for all he knew. Time had no meaning. But he became aware of Taylor's hands stroking his back, his arms. She shifted under him, wedging her hands between them. She mumbled something but he couldn't make out the words.

It took more strength than he realized to lift his head, and even then he only managed to move it an inch or two. "What?"

"I—can't—breathe."

Charles blinked, the words finally registering. He heaved himself off her, rolling to the side with a low groan. He heard her suck in a deep breath, felt the mattress shift under her weight as she settled more closely beside him. He draped one arm around her shoulders and pulled her against his side, his pulse kicking up a notch when she rested her head on his chest and snuggled closer.

He needed to get up. Dispose of the condom. Clean up. And then he should probably go home. He doubted Taylor actually wanted him to spend the night here.

He knew all that, but he couldn't make himself move. Not yet. In a few minutes, after his body recuperated.

That was all he needed, just a few minutes.

chapter NINE

The soles of his shoes made a soft shuffling noise against the carpet of the hallway, the sound too loud in the unnatural quiet that hung over the office area. Charles told himself he was only imagining the deathly silence, that the building was supposed to be quiet because it was still early.

The perfect time of day to make his getaway. There would be fewer witnesses to his humiliation when Murphy fired him.

That was why he was here so early, instead of still sleeping with Taylor's warm body curled against his. Guilt crept in at the way he'd left, without even waking her to tell her he was leaving. But she had looked so peaceful, so content, not even stirring when he leaned over to brush a kiss against the soft skin of her sleep-flushed cheek. Maybe he should have left her a note—

No, she'd understand. She knew he had to come here and face the music, clean out the few personal belongings tucked away in his desk. To leave his notes and marketing plan with Murphy. Charles hadn't been able to make it work, but maybe someone else could.

Yeah. Maybe. And maybe he'd develop real talent as a hockey player, too.

He swallowed back a bitter laugh and headed toward the tiny cubicle, eager to just get everything over with and leave. After that, he'd go home, tweak his resume, then call Taylor and see if she wanted to go to lunch or dinner or something.

"I didn't expect you in so early."

Murphy's voice echoed in the surrounding silence, catching Charles by surprise. He whirled around and faced the older man, bracing himself for the firing he knew was coming.

Murphy stepped closer, his gaze raking Charles from the tip of his old shoes to the collar of his stretched-out sweatshirt. He hadn't bothered to go home to change, not when he knew he wasn't going to be here for long.

Murphy's gaze met his, his gray brows shooting up in surprise. "I didn't realize today was Casual Friday."

"I wasn't staying long. I just—" Charles stopped, the older man's words finally registering.

"Were you planning on going somewhere?"

"I thought—"

"Because we've got a lot to go over, especially after the piece that ran last night."

"Yeah, about that." Charles shifted his weight from one foot to the other and glanced over his shoulder, grateful the office was still empty. "I had no idea it was going to be like that. And I understand that you'll want to bring in someone new. I was just going to clear my things out and leave."

"Why?"

Charles hesitated, wondering what the older man was up to. Did he expect Charles to do a few more things before firing him? Or was he just dragging things out, drawing out the inevitable?

"I figured after last night's piece, you'd be looking for someone else to handle the team's marketing."

Murphy laughed, the sound too loud in the silence. "Hell no, son. Why would I do something like that?"

"Did you happen to see the piece last night?"

Murphy leaned against a cubicle wall and folded his arms in front of him. "I did. Not exactly what I had been hoping for. I doubt it was what you were hoping for, too. Doesn't mean I'm ready to throw you to the wolves. Not yet."

"But—"

"Have you checked the reports this morning?"

"No. I didn't—"

"Maybe you should. We sold 176 tickets after the piece ran. Doesn't sound like a lot, but that pushed us over the halfway mark."

"That's still a long way from what I hoped."

"Maybe. But it's better than I expected."

Charles blinked, wondering if he had heard correctly. "Better?"

"Hell, Chuck. You didn't seriously think we'd sell out the first game, did you?"

"I had hoped—"

Murphy cut him off with a quick wave of his hand. "Yeah, it would be nice. Damn nice. But it's not realistic. I would have been happy with a few hundred tickets sold. It's a new league. A new team. Something completely different. I'm not expecting a miracle overnight. None of us are."

"But I thought that's what you wanted. That you brought me onboard for that."

"I did." Murphy smiled again and leaned forward, a glint in his shrewd eyes. "But not for the first game. No, as nice as that would be, I'm not expecting it. Now, by the final game of the season? Yeah, I want those seats filled. We've got all season to work toward that. If you do your job—and if the girls do theirs—then we can make it happen."

"By the end of the season?"

"That's the idea. Unless you're planning on going somewhere. Are you?"

"What? Oh. No." Charles shook his head, not only in response to the question, but to clear the disbelief that was running through his mind. "No, I'm not going anywhere."

"Good. That piece last night gave us a boost. I expect you to capitalize on it and go from there." Murphy pushed away from the wall then reached into the pocket of his suit. He pulled out a crumpled piece of paper and held it out toward Charles.

"What's this?"

"The number to the Banners' marketing office. I got a phone call last night from someone over there. Seems the piece caught their attention last night and they want to talk to you."

Charles stared at the familiar number, excitement mingling with frustration. He'd been calling that same number for two weeks, only to be placed on hold or brushed off. So why the sudden change? Was it the news piece from last night? Or did it have more to do with Sonny LeBlanc and JP Larocque? Unlike Taylor, Charles didn't care. He'd use whatever advantage he could to get his job done.

Especially now that it looked like he still had a job.

He curled his fingers around the crumpled slip of paper and glanced back at Murphy. "I'll call them as soon as the office opens."

"Good. Let me know what they say. And Chuck?"

"Yeah?"

"I don't have a problem with Casual Fridays but next time, maybe you want to make sure you don't look like you just rolled out of bed."

Heat filled his face as he ran a quick hand through his mussed hair. Murphy just laughed and walked away, leaving him standing there.

Stunned.

Surprised.

Shocked.

He'd walked in fifteen minutes ago, expecting to be out of a job, only to learn that things were picking up. He still had work to do—a lot of work. Maybe Murphy was happy with the way things had gone so far, but Charles certainly wasn't. Not by a long shot.

And now that he knew he still had a job, it was time to put the second phase of his plan into motion. Would it work? Who the hell knew. But it certainly couldn't be any worse than yesterday's fiasco.

He spun on his heel and headed to the small cubicle he called an office, his mind already racing ahead and making plans.

chapter TEN

Sweat covered her face, dripping into her eyes with a sting that made the breath hitch in her lungs. Taylor ignored the burning and kept pushing. Harder, faster, the puck cradled against the blade of the stick. She moved down the ice, spun and darted to the left then cut back to the right, darting away from Rachel Woodhouse. She heard the other woman mutter under her breath, calling her a bitch as Taylor left her behind.

Her lips curled in a cold smile, just a quick one as she pulled back with the stick and sent the puck flying. It hit the back of the net with a satisfying *whoosh* and Taylor smiled again.

No, it didn't count. The net was empty and this was nothing more than practice, but it still felt good. The sweat. The stretching and burning of muscles. The cut of blades slicing across the ice as her legs moved beneath her.

She was at home on the ice. Comfortable. Relaxed.

It was where she belonged.

And it was exactly what she needed to work out her frustrations after yesterday morning, when she woke up.

Alone.

She circled around the net then leaned down and grabbed the puck. Her eyes darted to the left, resting on the solitary figure sitting on the bleachers. Her stomach did a slow roll when their gazes met and she looked away as heat rushed to her face.

Or maybe she had only imagined meeting his gaze. Maybe he wasn't looking at her at all.

And maybe she was the world's biggest fool for jumping into bed with him the other night. God, what had she been thinking? She didn't do things like that. Ever. She could count her limited number of partners on one hand—with fingers left over. And she had never had a one-night stand. Never ever.

Until the night before last with Chuckie.

What the hell was he doing here, anyway? No, he hadn't been fired—she had learned that this morning before practice started. But it was a Saturday morning. Shouldn't he be somewhere else, doing whatever it is he usually did?

Coach Reynolds blew the whistle and stepped out to the ice, waving everyone in. Taylor yanked her helmet off and headed toward center ice. Rachel slid up next to her, anger simmering in her blue eyes.

"You're not as good as you think you are, LeBlanc." Her voice was pitched low, laced with venom and dislike. Taylor clenched her jaw and did what she always tried to do: ignore her.

Rachel grabbed her arm, her grip a little too hard. "You shouldn't even be playing on this team, not after the embarrassment you caused the other night with the media."

Don't say anything. Don't say anything.

Rachel moved closer, her face only inches away, her mouth twisted in a sneer. "And you sure as hell don't deserve that C."

Taylor had seen that one coming. The only surprising thing was that it had taken Rachel this long to say anything. She had seen the woman's face this morning when Coach Reynolds had made the announcement, naming Taylor as Team Captain and Sammie and Maddison as Alternates. Rachel had been livid, her face turning an unbecoming shade of red. Taylor was surprised the woman hadn't thrown a hissy fit right then and there.

But Rachel was too smart for that. She would have drawn the ire of the coaching staff if she had said or done anything.

So why was she doing it now, when Coach Reynolds was watching them?

"Let it go, Rach."

"No. It's bullshit. We both know the only reason you're even on this team is because of your last name."

"Whatever." Taylor jerked her arm from the woman's grasp and started to move away. Rachel grabbed her again, spinning her around.

And snapping Taylor's last nerve.

She tossed her helmet and stick to the ice and moved forward, fast, shoving her shoulder into Rachel's chest. The move caught Rachel by surprise and she stumbled back, her arms pinwheeling for balance. Taylor reached out and curled her hand in the woman's jersey, catching her before she fell. Then she yanked Rachel forward until they were nose-to-nose.

"I'm on this team because I'm good. Damn good. I have no idea what the fuck your problem is but you need to get over it. We're supposed to be on the same fucking—"

The shrill blare of a whistle sounding in her ear interrupted her. Taylor glanced to the right, not surprised to see Coach Reynolds standing right next to them.

And she was pissed.

Taylor released her hold on Rachel's jersey and stepped back, her jaw clenched so tight that her back teeth actually hurt. Silence descended over the rink, thick and uncomfortable. Was everyone watching them? Of course they were. Why wouldn't they be? They were squared off at center ice, looking like two combatants ready to tear each other apart.

Coach stared at both of them, her face a mask of anger and impatience—and disappointment. The silent scrutiny went on for so long that Taylor started fidgeting on the ice, anxious for Coach to dish out whatever punishment she was going to deliver.

"Laps. Both of you."

Rachel glanced over her shoulder then looked back at the coach. "But—"

"Now. I'll tell you when to stop." Coach spun around and walked away. Taylor muttered under her breath and retrieved her equipment from the ice. Rachel spun toward her, her face red with anger.

"This is all your fault, you stupid bitch."

"Whatever, Rach."

"I have somewhere I need to be."

"Then start skating."

"If it weren't for you—"

"You know something, Rach? I'm sick and tired

of your attitude. Maybe if you learned to keep your mouth shut, shit like this wouldn't happen."

"But—" Rachel's mouth snapped closed as she blinked, then blinked again. And oh shit, was she getting ready to cry? It sure as hell looked like it.

Taylor hesitated. Rachel was too hard, definitely not the kind of woman to cry. Then again, she *was* the kind of woman who would stop at nothing to get her way.

Whatever. Not her problem. Taylor dropped the helmet onto her head then started moving around the boards, her stride long and steady and slow. Rachel finally moved in next to her, anger rolling off her in waves.

Coach's voice rang out across the ice. "Pick it up ladies. I want to see some speed in that stride."

Taylor groaned, the sound echoed by Rachel. She gritted her teeth and pushed forward, picking up her pace as she rounded the boards.

How many laps? How long before Coach took pity on them and let them stop? Five? Eight? Twelve? Taylor lost count, could focus on nothing more than putting one skate in front of the other.

On her chest, heaving to draw air.

On her legs, burning with fatigue.

On her eyes, stinging with the sweat dripping into them.

The whistle finally blew, ending the agony with one short blast. Taylor bent over at the waist, her stick braced against her legs, and glided to a stop. She wanted to drop to the ice and simply collapse but that wasn't an option—she needed to stretch. To cool down. To rehydrate.

But not yet, not when Coach stepped onto the ice

and faced both of them, the expression of anger still clear on her face.

"Now do either one of you want to tell me what the hell is going on with you two?"

Taylor exchanged an uncertain glance with Rachel before they both shook their heads and answered in unison.

"No, Coach."

"You're both on the same team. I need you to remember that. And to start acting like it. Is that clear?"

"Yes, Coach."

"I've got enough to worry about without two of my players going at each other every chance they get." Coach Reynolds brushed the light brown hair off her face and leveled a biting glare at Rachel. "Woodhouse, get off your high horse and accept that LeBlanc is on this team because of her skill, not her name. Whatever petty jealousy is lurking inside that blonde head of yours needs to go away. Is that clear?"

Rachel slid a tense glance at Taylor, gritted her teeth, and nodded. "Yes, Coach."

Coach turned her anger on Taylor. "LeBlanc, I gave you that C because you deserved it. Don't make me regret it. Start acting like a leader. Understood?"

Taylor swallowed, the heat of embarrassment filling her already-flushed face. "Yes, Coach."

Coach stared at both of them for a long minute then finally stepped to the side. "Both of you, get out of here."

They both headed toward the door, their pace even until they reached it. Taylor sensed Rachel's hurry and moved to the side, letting her pass. The woman tossed her a glance, one filled with anger and worry, then pushed past Taylor and practically ran to the locker room.

"Gee, you're welcome." Taylor muttered the words under her breath and stepped off the ice, only to come to a sudden halt when Chuckie pushed away from the boards and stopped right in front of her. He held a bottle of water out in a silent offer.

Taylor almost walked right past him—she wasn't in the mood to deal with him right now, not after those grueling laps. But the water was too tempting to pass up so she grabbed it from his hand, uncapped it, and downed half in one long swallow. She wiped her mouth with the back of her hand then gave him a curt nod.

"Thanks." She started to step around him but he moved, blocking her.

"Remind me to never piss off a coach."

"Yeah."

"You look beat."

"You think?" She shifted her weight from one skate to the other then blew out a deep sigh. "Was there something you wanted, Chuckie?"

"Just wondering if you wanted to grab something to eat."

"All I want to do is shower and pass out." She hesitated, frowning. "Alone."

Confusion flashed in his eyes. His brows lowered in a frown and he leaned closer. The frown turned into a grimace and he quickly stepped back. Taylor tried to swallow the laughter that threatened to break free but couldn't, not at the look of horror that crossed Chuckie's face when he realized what he'd done.

"Yeah, pretty ripe, huh?"

His face turned an even deeper red. "I didn't mean—"

"It's not a big deal. I'd do the same. Which is why

I really need to hit the shower."

"And then we can grab something to eat?"

"Why?"

"What do you mean, why? Because you need food. And because I wanted to talk."

"About what? The other night?" A brief spurt of anger flared inside. "Or maybe about how you disappeared afterward?"

"I didn't—" He stopped midsentence, his mouth snapping shut at her frown. "Okay, I screwed up. You can beat me up for it over lunch."

"Not in the mood."

"Sure you are. You're just being stubborn."

"I don't want—"

"And after you beat me up, I have something I want to run by you."

"Not interested."

"Don't care. Go, hit the shower. I'll wait for you."

"Chuckie, I'm not going to lunch with you." But she was talking to air because Chuckie had already stepped around her, heading toward Coach Reynolds. Taylor hesitated then finally shook her head and started toward the locker room. Let him wait all he wanted. She still wasn't going with him.

Even if she was curious about what he wanted to run by her.

chapter ELEVEN

The diner was surprisingly empty. Or maybe not so surprising, considering it was early Saturday afternoon, well past the normal lunch time. If Charles had known how empty it would be, he would have picked a different place.

Like maybe the busy airport. Or a train station. Or hell, even the food court in the mall. At least then, there'd be noise and conversation. Not theirs, of course, not with the way Taylor was sitting across from him.

Toying with her food.

Not saying a word.

He reached for the glass of soda and took a quick sip, then sat the glass back on the table. Maybe a little too hard, because the *thunk* echoed around them. Taylor glanced up, raised her brows in silent question, then moved her attention back to her nearly-empty plate.

Still not saying a word.

For a lunch date, it was less-than-successful. *Failure* was actually a more appropriate description. Not that this was really a date but still—

"How was your food?"

Taylor glanced up, her eyes carefully blank, and shrugged. "Fine. For the dozenth time."

Had he asked her that already? He must have, but damned if he remembered. Trying to draw her into conversation was like pulling teeth—from a lion. Or maybe lioness was a better word.

He pushed his cleared plate away, ran the napkin over his mouth, then balled it up and tossed it on the table. "So what's going on with you and Woodhouse?"

"Nothing."

"Didn't look like nothing to me. I thought you were getting ready to flatten her on the ice."

"Nope."

"Maybe I need my eyes checked, then."

"Probably." Taylor pushed her plate away with a soft sigh then looked to the left, her gaze darting out the large plate glass window next to their booth. Traffic on York Road was busy, filled with cars moving north and southbound. He glanced out the window, his eyes squinting against the bright sun.

The day was too nice to be spent inside. Crisp and clear, the air tinged with the scent and feel of autumn. In another week or two, you'd need a jacket to go outside. Maybe—October in Maryland could change in the blink of an eye. But today was one of those rare days, filled with sun and a clear blue sky and no hint of humidity. It was a day to be spent outdoors, not inside a mostly-empty diner trying to have a conversation with someone who obviously had no desire to talk.

"So what do you normally do on the weekends?"

Taylor's gaze shifted from the heavy traffic to him. Impatience flashed in her eyes, quickly replaced by resignation. "Practice on Saturdays. Family dinner on Sundays. Then get ready for work during the week."

"I don't think I realized you worked."

"Of course I work. Why wouldn't I?"

"I just didn't think—"

"Newsflash for you, Chuckie. We *all* work. Everyone has another job. This hockey thing? It doesn't pay squat. It's, like, one step up from a beer league."

"That could change, you know."

"Really?" The disbelief was clear in her eyes. "Excuse me if I don't hold my breath."

"You know, for someone who wants to play hockey more than anything else in the world, your attitude pretty much sucks."

"My attitude does *not* suck!"

"Yeah? Then what do you call it?"

"Being realistic."

"Your definition is obviously different from mine."

"I have a feeling your reality is a bit different than mine."

Charles leaned back and studied her for a long minute—maybe too long because she shifted on the bench and looked away. He released a sigh and took another sip of his soda. "Listen, it's the first year. Hell, the season hasn't even officially started yet. And I know the pay isn't exactly the greatest—"

"The greatest? Do you even know what we're getting paid?"

"Well, no, but—"

Taylor propped her elbows on the table and leaned forward, interrupting him with the force of her whiskey-gaze. "A couple hundred a game, at the most. And that's not even everyone. We don't get paid for our two practices a week. We have to pay for our own equipment and jerseys. So don't sit there and try to put a sunshine-and-roses marketing twist on it, okay? It's not going to work, not when I know damn well you don't have to worry about a second job to make ends meet."

Charles looked down, wondering if the surprise he felt showed on his face. Yes, he had known the girls weren't making a lot of money, but he hadn't known the extent of it. Guilt crept over him and he pushed it away. "I didn't realize—"

"Yeah, no kidding."

"Taylor—"

"Just drop it, okay? You said you wanted to run something by me. What was it?"

He started to brush her off, to tell her he wanted to keep this particular conversation going. An idea was already forming in his mind, one that might help. But he snapped his mouth closed, thinking better of it at the last minute. It was just a small idea, one that wasn't completely formed. And it wasn't something he could manage on his own—he'd need some outside help. No sense in even bringing it up, since he wasn't sure it would ever come to fruition.

He drained the soda then leaned across the table. "I'm trying to work something out with the Banners. I had a nice conversation with the head of their marketing group yesterday."

Taylor watched him through narrowed eyes filled with suspicion. A long minute went by, filled with heavy silence, before she finally spoke.

"This isn't going to be like that fiasco from Thursday night, is it?"

Hurt, unexpected and unwelcome, flashed through him. For a brief second, he was the lonely, awkward kid again, uncomfortable and completely out of his league. *Fiasco?* Is that what she thought Thursday night had been? Then he realized she was talking about the news piece that had aired, not about what had happened between them.

They hadn't talked about what happened between them at all. Should they? Should he bring it up? He hesitated then gave himself a mental shake as he made his decision: he'd take his cue from Taylor, and right now, she didn't seem to want to talk about it.

"Well? Is it?"

"No." Charles shook his head. "No, it won't be anything like what happened Thursday night. Trust me."

"Trust you? After what happened?"

"I had no control over it. And if I had known what was going to happen—"

"You wouldn't have shown up at my place, right?"

"What?"

Taylor shook her head and looked away, suddenly focused on the smooth edge of her thumbnail. "Nothing."

"We're talking about the news piece that aired, right?"

Her gaze darted to his then slid away. "Yeah. Of course."

"Okay. Because if we're talking about something else—"

"There's nothing else to talk about."

"Are you sure? Because I thought—"

Taylor sliced her hand through the air with an impatient wave. "So what about the Banners?"

"It's too late for next weekend, but we're talking about setting up a small demonstration. Maybe for the beginning of November."

"What kind of demonstration?"

"The Blades would play a quick scrimmage on the ice during one of the intermissions. We'd set up an autograph session afterward, try to tap into the Banners' market and increase interest."

A thoughtful frown crossed Taylor's face. "A scrimmage? You mean, like the Mites do sometimes?"

"Well, yeah. I guess. Something like that." Charles watched her, trying to gauge her thoughts on the idea. But her face was carefully blank—too blank. He held his breath, wondering what faults she might find with the idea.

Another long minute stretched around them. Taylor's face relaxed as a gleam of interest flashed in her eyes. "I think that might be fun. Maybe. I mean, it certainly couldn't hurt, right?"

It wasn't the most enthusiastic response, but he'd take it. Charles smiled and sat back. "Great. I'll call them on Monday and get things set up."

"Why didn't you just set it up yesterday while you were talking to them?"

"I wanted to run it by you first."

"Why? It's not up to me. You're the PR Director or whatever."

"Yeah. But you're the team Captain. I wanted to make sure I had your support first."

"Why?"

"Because whether you realize it or not, you have

some influence over the ladies. If you decided to have a major attitude problem over this, it would have made my job a lot harder."

"I don't have a major attitude."

Charles laughed, the sound quick and deep. "The hell you don't. What about all the grief you gave me the last few weeks?"

"That wasn't attitude."

"What do you call it?"

"I call it not liking being used. Me or my family. And that whole thing didn't exactly turn out great, did it?"

His amusement quickly faded. "I told you, I had no control—"

"Yeah. I know." Taylor leaned across the bench seat and grabbed her backpack. "Want to know what would be really impressive?"

"What?"

"Set up an exhibition game between the Blades and the Banners. Now *that* would be awesome."

"I'm not sure—"

"Yeah, I know. Whatever. Just an idea." She slid off the bench and tossed the backpack over her shoulder.

"Where are you going?"

"Home. I have stuff to do."

"But we're still having lunch."

"No we're not. See? Plates are empty."

"That doesn't mean you have to run off. I thought we could—" His voice drifted off, the words dying in his throat at the questioning look on her face. He glanced away, cleared his throat, then looked back at Taylor. "Did you want to grab dinner tonight maybe?"

"Can't. I'm babysitting the twins."

"What about tomorrow?"

"Can't do that either. A few of us are going to RennFest tomorrow." She hoisted the strap of the backpack higher on her shoulder then offered him a quick smile. "Thanks for lunch, Chuckie. I'll see later."

Charles turned on the bench, stunned at her abrupt departure. What the hell had just happened? He thought about calling out to her but it was too late, she was already pushing her way through the diner doors.

Charles watched her leave, wondering if he had missed something. Should he have brought up what happened between them? Is that why she had left so quickly? Did she really have plans, or was she just making excuses?

If it had been any other woman, he would have known exactly what to say or do. How to romance and wine-and-dine and sweet talk her. But it wasn't any other woman—it was Taylor. And even now, even after being with her, she still managed to tie him up in knots and confuse the living hell out of him.

He turned back around and signaled the waitress for the check, his mind sorting through options on how to deal with Taylor LeBlanc. He wanted to see her again. Be with her again. But he had no idea if Taylor was even interested. He had thought she was, but now he wasn't so sure.

Then again, when it came to Taylor, he was never sure about anything.

chapter TWELVE

"So tell me about the hottie."

Taylor slid a sideways glance at Sammie and pretended she had no idea what she was talking about. "What hottie?"

"Don't play stupid. You know who—Clare, no, put that down." Sammie lunged two steps and grabbed the crumpled paper her daughter had picked up from the ground and was ready to put in her mouth. The toddler's face scrunched up in dismay and her wide hazel eyes filled with moisture. Sammie blew out a quick breath and rolled her eyes. "Don't even start, young lady. You're not fooling me at all."

Clare's round face smoothed out as she studied her mother for a few long seconds. Then she blinked and looked away, her gaze already focusing on something else as she started walking again. Taylor caught up to the pair, laughing.

"Don't encourage her. Honestly, she's going to be

a drama queen when she gets older. I have no idea where she gets it from."

Taylor raised her brows in amusement, earning her a half-hearted scowl from Sammie. "You don't? Really?"

"Ha ha. I am *not* a drama queen. Not even close."
"Maybe."

"No *maybe* about it." Sammie kept her gaze on Clare as they moved through the crowds, side-stepping people dressed in costumes ranging from knights to wenches. One woman carrying a basket of lollipops stopped next to Clare with a wide smile on her face.

"Well aren't you just the most adorable little thing?" The woman grabbed a lollipop from the basket and bent over, holding it out to Clare. The movement exposed an even larger portion of her abundant cleavage, drawing attention from others moving around them.

"Oh, good Lord." Sammie muttered the words under her breath and stepped forward, accepting the lollipop from the woman. Taylor bit back a laugh as a blush stained Sammie's cheeks when the wench gave her a thorough head-to-toe look then offered her a bright smile.

Sammie's blush deepened and she shook her head, grabbing Clare's hand and moving away from the woman after muttering something. Taylor caught up to them again, her laughter finally breaking free.

"It's not funny. I think that's the most action I've gotten in two years. And oh, good Lord, were those things really real?"

Taylor glanced over her shoulder, watching as the wench started flirting with two couples leaning against a tree. "Well, they're jiggling. Does that mean anything?"

"Stop staring!" Sammie smacked her on the elbow and kept walking.

"I wasn't staring! Well, okay, maybe a little. But how can you not, with the way everyone is dressed? I mean, I know it's all part of the festivities and everything but still. That can't be comfortable, with everything hanging out like that."

"Actually, it's not that bad." Sammie's eyes widened and she tossed a panic-stricken look at Taylor. "I mean—"

"Oh no. You're not getting out of that one." Taylor grabbed Sammie's arm and steered her off the leaf-strewn dirt lane, out of the way of foot traffic. "Are you telling me you've actually dressed up like that?"

"No. I mean, not really." Sammie squirmed then blew a dark curl off her forehead. "Okay, maybe once. In a totally different lifetime. And not as a wench. I was an elf."

"A what?" Taylor could barely manage to get the words out because she was laughing so hard.

"You heard me: an elf. An elven princess, to be exact. I even had this cool little bow I carried around."

"You were an elf? Seriously?"

"Yes. I mean, look at me." Sammie waved her free hand up and down, from the top of her curly dark hair to the toes of her dainty feet. "I made a perfect elf. Even my ears are pointy."

"Your ears are not pointy."

"Sure they are. See?" She brushed the thick curls away from her face and turned her head to the side, exposing a perfectly normal-looking rounded ear.

"Hmm. And how much alcohol had been involved?"

Sammie let her hair drop back into place and shrugged. "I plead the fifth."

"The fifth, huh? Of what? Tequila?"

"Not funny." She bent down and picked up Clare, resting the toddler on her hip as they started walking again. "You hungry, Boo?"

"Starving."

"I wasn't talking to you."

"I know. But I'm still starving. How about some steak-on-a-stake?"

"I was thinking more along the lines of one of those soup bread bowls."

Taylor glanced around then led the way to a row of rustic booths. "We can do both. And maybe some mead to wash it down with."

"Sounds like a perfect plan." Sammie glanced at her watch as they got in line then frowned. "Where's Shannon and Dani? I thought they were going to meet us here."

"They are. Probably stuck in traffic. You know how crazy it is trying to get into this place."

"True. And it's perfect weather this weekend, too, which makes it even worse."

Taylor nodded her agreement then looked around, studying the crowd gathered around them. She loved RennFest, always had. There was something about the atmosphere—the costumes, the make-believe, the revelry—that always made her feel lighter. Rejuvenated somehow. She didn't understand it and couldn't even begin to explain it, but she didn't need to—especially not here, where everyone was welcome to be themselves, and even encouraged to become someone different, at least for a little while.

"So are you going to tell me about him?"

Taylor paused her people-watching to glance at Sammie. "Who?"

"The hottie. Our PR Director. Mr. Dawson."

"*Mr. Dawson?*" Taylor laughed. "You mean Chuckie? Nothing to tell."

"Really? Because I've seen the way he looks at you. I'm surprised the ice didn't melt at practice yesterday."

Taylor pretended to study the hand-lettered menu board and prayed her face wasn't turning bright red. "Oh please. You're imagining things."

"Like I'm imagining that blush on your face?"

"Must be sunburn or something."

"You're too funny. Now come on, fess up. What's going on?"

"Nothing."

"So nothing happened between you two?"

"What? No. Of course not."

"You sure about that?"

"I would know, wouldn't I?"

"Yeah. Unless you wanted to hide it. Which is fine if you did, as long you didn't hide it from me."

"I'm not—"

"Because you know I'm living my life through you, right? So if you have something exciting to share, you should really share it."

Taylor hesitated, the urge to tell Sammie everything—well, almost everything—stronger than she had thought it would be. Something stopped her at the last minute, though. It wasn't that she didn't want to talk to someone about it—it was that she couldn't. Not yet. She had no idea what was going on, or if anything really was going on. They'd slept together. Once. That didn't mean anything, especially since stupid Chuckie hadn't even brought it up. Did that mean he regretted it already? Had it been nothing more than a one-night stand?

Maybe she *should* talk to Sammie about it, just to get her opinion. No, she couldn't. Not yet, not until she figured out what was going on. But knowing Sammie, she wouldn't let it drop, so Taylor had to find a way to change the subject.

Easy enough.

The line inched closer to the counter, but still far enough away that it would be a few minutes before it was their turn. Taylor brushed the hair out of her face then grinned at Sammie.

"You don't have to live your life through me, you know. There's nothing stopping you from living your own."

The smile on Sammie's face dimmed and she suddenly became preoccupied with smoothing her hand over Clare's thick brown hair. "It's a little different when you have a kid."

"I know. But not impossible. And I know you've had guys ask you out."

"It's not that easy—"

"All you have to do is say yes. I can always watch Clare if your parents can't."

"There hasn't been anyone I want to say *yes* to, so it's a moot point."

"I call bull—" Taylor stopped, glanced down at Clare, and cleared her throat. "Baloney. What about that one teacher you were telling me about? Didn't you say he asked you out for coffee?"

"Chris? Yes, he did. But I'm not interested. And that whole workplace romance thing isn't a good idea, anyway."

"It's just for coffee. You should go. You might

have fun."

"No, I think I'll pass."

"You know you're going to have to start dating eventually. You can't just shut yourself off from everything. It's been two years—"

"Taylor, I know you mean well, but it's not going to happen. I'm not ready. I'm not interested. And I already have a full life." Sammie leaned down and pressed a quick kiss against her daughter's forehead. "I have Clare. I have teaching. And I have the Blades and you guys. I don't need anything else."

Taylor wanted to argue but she knew better. This wasn't the first time they had had this conversation, and it wouldn't be the last. Taylor just wanted her friend to be happy—and pining over her ex-husband wasn't making her happy. She just wished there was something else she could do to help Sammie move forward.

They finally reached the counter and placed their orders, then stepped to the side to wait. A few minutes later, Taylor was balancing the overloaded tray as she followed Sammie through the crowd toward an empty table.

"Did you want to go get your mead?"

"No, I'll wait until after we eat. I don't feel like waiting in another line while my food gets cold." Taylor placed the tray on the table then swung her leg over the side of the bench. Sammie settled Clare next to her then dug into the large crossbody bag and pulled out a small sippy cup. She poured some juice into the cup, recapped it, then handed it to Clare as Taylor divided the plates between them.

"Are you getting nervous about next Saturday?"

Taylor looked up, surprised to see a faint hint of

anxiety in Sammie's deep brown eyes. "Nervous? Not really. Why? Are you?"

"Maybe. A little. I don't really know what to expect, you know?"

"Just keep reminding yourself it's nothing more than a game."

"Easier said than done." Sammie ripped a piece from the bread bowl, dragged it through the stew, then popped into her mouth.

"Why? You've played in games before."

"Yeah, but not like this. I was just playing in a co-ed beer league. No pressure. This is an actual *game*. In front of paying spectators."

"True." Taylor tipped her head to the side and bit off a piece of the thinly-sliced steak that had been speared on a skewer. It was well-done and not as seasoned as she normally liked, but it was still good. She swallowed and reached for the cup of soda and took a quick sip. "But you can't think of it that way. Besides, you won't even notice the crowd once the game starts. It just kind of fades into the background."

"Hmm." Sammie didn't look like she believed her but she didn't say anything else, just helped Clare with a few bites of her own food.

"What do you think about the idea of everyone going out after Saturday's game? As a celebration kind of thing."

"What if we lose?"

"Oh geez. Way to think positive, Reigler. Of course we're going to win."

"Spoken like a true pro."

"Not hardly." *Not even close. Not yet. Maybe not ever.* Taylor pushed the morose thought away and forced a grin to her face. "And even if something happens and we don't win, I think we should still go out. Like a bonding thing."

"Sounds like a plan to me. I'll make sure my parents can take Clare home after the game." Sammie glanced down at her daughter then frowned and grabbed a napkin to wipe the girl's chubby fingers. She looked back at Taylor with the same frown on her face.

"What?"

"You have steak sauce dribbling down your chin."

"Do I? Gah." Taylor reached for a napkin then froze at the voices behind her. She knew all three of them, but it was only one that sent something like panic shooting through her.

She spun around on the bench, a napkin clutched in one hand and her half-eaten steak-on-a-stake clutched in the other. Shannon Wiley and Dani Baldwin slid to a stop next to their table, but Taylor wasn't paying any attention to them.

It was the man behind them that caught her eye. Tall, lean, wearing faded denim jeans and a long-sleeve Henley shirt, the sleeves pushed up his forearms. Dark stubble covered his sculpted jaw. The corner of his mouth curled up in a dangerous grin and his ocean blue eyes sparkled with humor as he looked at her.

Shannon dropped to the bench next to Taylor and reached around her, stealing Taylor's soda. She took a long sip, belched the tiniest bit, then hooked a thumb over her shoulder towards Chuckie.

"Look who we found walking around." Shannon took another long sip through the straw then leaned forward, her brows lowered over her brown eyes as she studied Taylor. "Did you know you've got sauce all over your chin?"

chapter
THIRTEEN

Taylor didn't want him there. She wasn't obvious about it, not in front of her teammates, but Charles still got the message loud and clear. He could see it in the narrowed looks she shot his way; in the set of her shoulders and chin whenever he said something.

In the way she kept angling herself so Sammie, Shannon, and Dani were between them.

The small group stopped at a booth that was creating wax hands. Sammie moved closer, a wistful expression on her face as she watched one couple dip their joined hands into a large vat of wax. She turned back and smiled.

"Isn't that so sweet? I'd love to do something like that."

Shannon snorted. "You're one hand short, genius. You need to have a boyfriend first."

"I wasn't talking about *me*. I meant for Clare. I think it would be so sweet to have her hand cast in wax."

"You can't." Dani pointed toward an elegantly lettered sign. "Says you have to be at least five."

"Oh." Disappointment filled the woman's face as she looked down at the little girl resting on her hip. "Oh well, Boo. Guess we have to wait two years, don't we?"

"You can probably find something like that at a craft store. They have all sorts of things like that." Taylor's eyes narrowed when she realized everyone was watching her. "What?"

"And how exactly would you know anything about all that arts-and-crafts stuff?"

Taylor shrugged, the action causing a long hank of her silky hair to fall across her cheek. She brushed it away and grinned. "Not me. My mom and Aunt Emily did something like that when the twins were all born. It was kind of cute."

"If you say so." Shannon reached into her back pocket and pulled out a crumpled flyer. "It's almost time for the sword swallower. Who wants to go?"

"Count me out." Sammie shifted Clare on her hip. "I don't think that would be the best thing for Clare to see. Might give her nightmares."

"And it might not." Shannon shoved the crumpled sheet back into her pocket then looked at Charles with a teasing gleam in her eyes. "How about you, Chuck? Up to seeing some guy deep throat some swords with me?"

Charles opened his mouth to respond then promptly snapped it shut, not having any idea how to even answer. He didn't need to because the other three women jumped in, immediately giving Shannon a hard time. The other woman merely laughed and rolled her eyes.

"Guys, relax. I was only teasing."

"One of these days, your teasing is going to get you into so much trouble."

"Not hardly."

"Yeah, it is. Trust me." Dani grabbed her by the arm and started leading her away. "I'll go with this one and keep her under control. Where are you guys going to be so we can meet up later?"

"I think I'm going to go home. Clare's getting tired and I think my arm is falling asleep."

Taylor looked surprised but simply nodded. "And I drove with Sammie, so I guess I'm leaving, too."

Sammie turned, her dark mop of short curls bouncing as she shook her head. "You should stay here, Taylor. You haven't even had your mead yet."

"No, I'm good. We can—"

"I'll take you home." Charles tried to ignore the expression of panic that crossed Taylor's face when she looked at him. But the expression wasn't there for long, disappearing as soon as she blinked.

"I don't think—"

"That would be a great idea." Sammie shifted the little girl on her hip. "Tell Aunt Taylor goodbye, Boo."

Taylor shot an unreadable look at Sammie then leaned forward and ruffled the girl's hair. "Have fun, kiddo. Make sure you keep your mom on her toes."

"Gee, thanks. I'll remember that."

"So, LeBlanc. Does that mean you'll be around for a while?"

Taylor shot a quick look at Charles then sighed, the sound long and loud. "Yeah, I guess. We'll catch up later."

Dani and Shannon turned identical speculative

glances in his direction. A sly smile crossed Shannon's face. "You need your head examined if you don't drag him home and—"

"Okay, enough. We're out of here." Dani dragged Shannon away, their laughter fading as they walked away. Charles shifted as heat washed over him. Not just the heat of embarrassment, but the heat of anticipation because that was exactly what he wanted to do: drag Taylor home.

He shoved his hands into the back pockets of his jeans and cleared his throat. "Remind me to make sure that woman never talks in front of a camera."

"Yeah, that would be a public relations nightmare for sure." Sammie smiled then leaned in close to Taylor and spoke, her words too low for him to hear. Whatever she said caused a faint blush to spread across Taylor's cheeks. Curiosity burned through him but he kept it in check, at least until Sammie walked away.

"What was that all about?"

"Hm?" Taylor glanced at him and quickly looked away with a shrug. "Nothing."

"Why don't I believe that?"

The flush on Taylor's cheeks deepened and she looked away. She shuffled her feet, kicking at some of the stray leaves littering the dirt path, then started walking away. Charles fell into step beside her, noticing the way she kept her gaze averted as they moved through the crowd.

"So. Did you want to get some mead? Or just walk around or—"

"Why are you here, Chuckie?"

His steps faltered. "What do you mean?"

"Just what I said. I know you didn't just happen to show up here. So why are you here?"

"Maybe I just wanted to come and people-watch."

"Yeah, right." Taylor stepped off the path, out of the flow of traffic, and leaned back against the trunk of an old gnarled tree. She crossed her arms in front of her, the action tugging the hem of the long-sleeved shirt up. Charles glanced down then looked away, trying to ignore the sight of firm flesh visible above the waistband of her loose jeans.

Taylor cocked a brow in his direction, impatience flaring in her eyes. "Well?"

"Well, what?"

"Why are you here?"

There was no sense in trying to convince her it was simply coincidence, not when she obviously knew better. He took a step closer, close enough that he could feel the heat of her body warming the air between them. He braced one hand against the trunk, just above her head, and leaned down so his face was mere inches from hers.

"Maybe I just wanted to see you."

Her eyes widened then just as quickly narrowed. "So you decided to follow me?"

Charles grinned and leaned a little closer. "Maybe."

"That's, uh—" Taylor shifted, her gaze darting to the side before meeting his. "That's a little stalkerish, don't you think?"

"No. Just determined."

"Why?"

"Because I figured this was the only way to see you."

"I saw you yesterday."

"Yeah. And you walked out like you couldn't get away fast enough."

"No I didn't. I just—" Her voice trailed off and she looked away again, frowning. Charles waited, wondering if she would duck under his arm and run away again. He held his breath, uncertainty eating at him until she finally looked back. The same uncertainty he felt glittered in her eyes as she watched him.

"So the other night wasn't just a thing?"

"A *thing*?"

"Yeah. Like, you know, a one-time-weak-moment thing."

"Is that what you want it to be?"

Taylor looked away again. A faint blush spread across her cheeks, growing a little redder with each passing second. His gaze drifted to her lower lip and he watched, enthralled, as she nibbled at the tender flesh. It would be so easy—so tempting—to close his mouth over hers. To nip her full lower lip. To show her exactly what he wanted.

But he didn't do any of that. He couldn't, not yet. Not until she answered the question. "Well? Is it?"

She turned back to him, the vulnerability in her eyes hitting him with the force of a hard punch in the gut. "No. I'm not—I've never done the whole one-time thing."

Relief seared him, easing the ache in his chest. Not just relief, but something else, something he didn't want to question just yet, let alone acknowledge. He grinned then brushed his mouth across hers, the lightest grazing of flesh against flesh. "Good."

He pushed away from her then reached down and wrapped his hand around hers. She tensed the slightest bit and Charles waited, wondering if maybe he had misunderstood, wondering if maybe she had meant she wasn't interested at all. But the tension left her and he swallowed a sigh of relief as her fingers finally curled around his. He tugged and led them back onto the path, falling into step with the throngs of merrymakers.

"So you said something about twins?"

"What?"

"Earlier. You said something about twins. Are they your cousins?"

"Yeah. And sisters." Taylor laughed and squeezed his hand when he stumbled. "*Two* sets of twins. My sisters, Mia and Cassie. They're eleven. And Aunt Emily and Uncle JP have twin girls, too. Madelina and Suzanne. They're both nine."

"Wow. I bet family dinners are a bit chaotic, huh? I take it twins run in the family?"

"Apparently."

"Good to know." This time it was Taylor who stumbled. Charles shot her a mischievous grin then led the way up the shadowed path toward the booths that sold alcohol. "Do they happen to play hockey, too?"

"A little. Mia and Suzanne are more into it than the other two, though."

"Well, I'm sure they're naturals. Kind of hard not to be, considering everyone in their family. Are they coming to the game next weekend?"

"Yup. Everyone's going to be there."

Charles glanced down at her, surprised at the sharp tension he heard in her voice. "You don't sound very excited."

Taylor's gaze dropped to her feet and she shrugged. "I am. It's just—"

"Just what?"

"I don't know. I guess I'm still a little disappointed, you know?"

"Why?"

"You know why. We had this discussion the other day."

He dropped her hand and wrapped his arm around her shoulder, pulling her closer. "It's the first season, Taylor. You've got to give it a chance. There's still plenty of time."

"But what if there's not? What if it totally bombs and completely sucks? What if the rumors are true and the league folds after the first few games?"

"Where in the hell did you hear that?"

"Oh please. We've been hearing that since the beginning."

"That's news to me. The league isn't going anywhere. The Blades aren't going anywhere."

"How can you be sure? You can't."

"You need to trust me, Taylor." He caught her gaze and held it, tried to force her to believe with nothing more than the strength of his own will. Hope flashed in her eyes, followed by disappointment.

"How do I know I can trust you, Chuckie?"

The words pierced him, as sharp and painful as if she had plunged a knife deep into his chest and twisted it. His body stiffened as a thousand different words and emotions flashed through him. Arguments. Comebacks. Reassurances.

Insecurities and doubts that made him feel like that awkward and inept kid from all those years ago.

Could Taylor see it? Sense it? No. She was already looking away, stepping closer to the counter to order. Still talking even though she wasn't looking at him, even though he wasn't really listening.

"I mean, are you even any good?"

Her final question penetrated the fog filling his mind. He stepped closer and frowned. "Any good?"

"Yeah." She looked over her shoulder at him as she pulled some bills from her back pocket. "I mean, you want me to trust you, but I don't even know if you're any good at what you do. I want to believe you are, or else Murph wouldn't have brought you on. But we thought the last guy was supposed to be good, too, and he's not around anymore."

She wasn't talking about trusting *him*, not personally. She was talking about trusting his marketing skills. An odd relief shot through him.

"I'm damn good at what I do, Taylor." He stopped her before she could pay for the drinks and pulled his own wallet out.

"Better than you were at playing hockey?"

Charles laughed, the sound rich and loud in the bustle surrounding them. He passed a few bills across the counter and accepted the two tall cups of mead, handing one to Taylor. He raised his own cup in a mock salute as he answered.

"A million times better."

Taylor watched him for a long minute, studying him so closely, he was tempted to fidget under her scrutiny. Then she smiled, her face lighting up as humor glittered in her eyes. She touched the rim of her cup against his.

"Well, that's something at least, right?"

chapter
FOURTEEN

Nerves fluttered in her stomach, making her fingers tremble and the breath hitch in her chest. It was stupid being nervous. But no matter how many times she told herself that, she couldn't stop the fluttering in her stomach.

Taylor finally jammed the key into the lock and turned it, then had to fight with it to get it back out as the door swung open. She glanced over her shoulder, a forced smile on her face as she looked at Chuckie. The smile died under the heat in his eyes as he watched her.

The fluttering in her stomach grew stronger. And God, this was so stupid. Why was she nervous? Chuckie was just being a gentleman by walking her to the door, that was all. It wasn't like he was going to jump her or anything.

Except maybe she wanted him to jump her. No, no *maybe* about it. That was exactly what she wanted.

Or maybe she should take charge and jump *him*. It wasn't like they hadn't already been together. They had.

Except this felt different for some reason. It didn't make sense, and Taylor was afraid to examine the reasons why. It was just sex, right? Sex after a nice day spent together, drinking mead and eating renaissance junk food and making merry with all the other revelers.

All she had to do was turn around, pull him inside, and kiss him. Press her body tight against his and let him know she wanted him. Easy enough, right? She shouldn't have any problems at all.

Except she couldn't even get her fingers to stop trembling long enough to get the stupid key out of the door. Taylor muttered under her breath and wiggled the key, trying to yank it out. She heard a soft chuckle behind her then jumped when Chuckie's hand closed over hers.

"Here, let me."

She stepped back, embarrassment sweeping over her as Chuckie eased the key from the lock with one smooth move. Great. Now she felt like an even bigger idiot.

He placed the keys into her hand then leaned against the door jamb, making no move to enter the apartment. She propped the door open with the toe of her shoe and tried to act sophisticated and worldly.

"You want to come in or something?" *Or something?* So much for sophisticated. What was wrong with her? This was *Chuckie*, for crying out loud. She shouldn't be this nervous or awkwardly shy around him.

Except he wasn't just *Chuckie*. Not anymore. Not after the other night. Not after today. The man in front of her bore no resemblance to the boy she remembered. Tall, broad. Lean and muscled. Dark hair, his strong jaw covered with the shadow of soft whiskers. And those eyes, so clear and deep a blue, filled with something close to amusement as he watched her.

And oh hell, who was she kidding? She hadn't thought of him as that annoying boy since after the first day she had seen him at practice. But something had changed in the last few days, something she didn't understand.

And she suddenly felt out of her league. Almost...intimidated.

Impatience swept through her. All she had to do was close the distance between them and kiss him. She wanted to. And she was pretty sure he wanted her to, as well. She could see it in the heat swirling beneath the amusement in his eyes as he watched her. So what was stopping her? Why was this so hard?

Her fingers tightened around the keys in her hand, the edges digging into the flesh of her palm as she narrowed her eyes at him. "Well? Do you?"

One corner of his mouth tilted up in a dangerous grin as he finally stepped past her. "How can I turn down an invitation like that?"

She frowned, wondering if he was making fun of her, then closed the door with a soft click. "You don't have to, you know."

Chuckie turned to face her, his body suddenly too close. "Don't have to what?"

"Uh, come in. If you don't want to, I mean."

"I'm already in."

"Yeah. I know. I just meant—if you didn't want to, you don't—" The rest of the words died in her throat as he stepped closer. Too close—yet not close enough. Nowhere near close enough. All she had to do was reach out and wrap her fist in his shirt, tug him a little bit closer, and kiss him. It should be easy enough to do. He was standing right there, within her reach.

But she couldn't do it and she didn't know why. It was all she could do to pull air into her lungs, to force herself to breathe so she wouldn't be quite so lightheaded.

"You look like you're about two seconds away from panicking."

Indignation shot through her, momentarily freeing her from the strange paralysis. "What? I do not! I never panic. I can't believe—"

"Taylor?" Chuckie's voice was deep and warm, almost too tantalizing to resist.

"Yeah?"

"Just do it."

And oh God, did he know what she wanted to do? But how? How could he tell? And did she really care?

No, not when he looked at her that way, with hunger flaring in the depths of those ocean blue eyes. She hesitated, but only for a second. Then she was reaching for him, the keys falling from her hand and hitting the floor with a loud jangle.

Her mouth crashed against his, hot and wet with hungry desperation. A part of her wondered at the desperation, questioned the wisdom of letting him know how much she wanted him. Then Chuckie's mouth opened under hers and she didn't care about anything except the heavy need sweeping over her.

She fisted her hands in the hem of his shirt and dragged it up, her knuckles grazing the hot flesh of smooth abs and broad chest. He groaned, the sound filled with need and hunger. It unleashed something inside her, freeing her.

Taylor broke the kiss long enough to pull the shirt over his head, then dragged her mouth along the side of his jaw. His hands tightened around her waist then slid down to cup her ass, holding her close as he rocked against her. Fire unfurled deep in her belly as she felt the hard length of his erection press against her and she suddenly wanted more.

Needed more.

Hunger, hot and almost desperate, exploded inside her, obliterating all doubt. All inhibition. She nipped his shoulder and dragged her short nails through the spattering of hair in the middle of his chest. Lower, down along the flat of his stomach to the waistband of his jeans. She reached for the button with trembling fingers, popped it open and tugged the zipper down then reached inside. Her fingers curled around the hard length of his cock, stroking him.

The breath caught in his chest, escaped on a long moan as his head fell back. Taylor watched him through glazed eyes, power washing over her as he clenched his jaw tighter with each stroke. *She* was doing this to him. *She* was the reason his chest rose and fell with deep gulping breaths. *She* was the reason his cock hardened even more in her hand.

She lowered her mouth and rained kisses along his chest, the heat of his flesh searing her lips. She ran her tongue across one flat nipple, heard his swift intake of breath and did it again. Lower, tracing the faint line of dark hair that ran down his stomach.

She released his hold him and dropped to her knees, grabbed the waistband of his jeans and tugged the denim down past his hips. She glanced up, watching him through heavy-lidded eyes as she took him into her mouth. He gasped then groaned, the sound long and deep and hungry as his hands curled into her hair.

"Taylor. Christ." His hips rocked in a slow rhythm as she pulled him deeper into her mouth. Licking, sucking. Harder. Faster. Spurred on by a hunger that burned deep and hot inside her. Making her want. Need. Crave.

His fingers tightened in her hair and she waited, anticipation of his climax spiraling deep inside her. She'd never done this before, not like this, had never *wanted* to before. But she wanted to now. More than she could have ever imagined.

But Chuckie pulled away, his breathing harsh and ragged. He leaned down, his mouth closing over hers as he pulled her to her feet. She sighed in disappointment then gasped in surprise when he pinned her against the door. He pulled her hands over her head and held them in place with one hand, his other moving down to undo her jeans. She shimmied against him, heat spiraling through her as he dragged her pants down. Then his hand dipped between her legs and his fingers slipped inside her and it was her turn to gasp.

"Christ, Tay-Tay. You're so fucking wet." His words were nothing more than a hoarse growl, filled with need and wonder. She moaned, unable to speak, unable to do anything but *feel* as his fingers slid in and out of her. Her hips moved, searching for more, silently begging.

Chuckie released her hands and bent forward, dragging the jeans and her underwear down her legs. He yanked off one shoe and sock, freed her leg, then stood back up as he reached behind him and pulled something out of his pocket.

A condom, she realized. He reached between them, sheathed himself, then stroked her clit and slid two fingers inside once more. Stroking, deep and hard, dragging her to the edge and holding her there with an unspoken promise of what was still to come.

Then his mouth was on hers again, hot and wet and demanding, his tongue thrusting against hers as he lifted her. She gasped in surprise, her fingers digging into his shoulders.

"Wrap your legs around me."

"But—"

"Now. Do it." His harsh command unleashed something deep inside her, some strange primal need she didn't understand. Taylor wrapped her legs around his waist, felt him lift her even higher.

And then he was inside her, stretching her, filling her. Deep, so deep. He drove into her, hard and fast. Her head dropped back against the door, her lungs aching with the need to draw air as he plunged into her over and over.

Her fingers dug deeper into his shoulders, clinging, searching for something to hold her steady as she rocked against him, meeting each thrust with a hunger she didn't understand. Sensation built deep inside, coiling, tightening, promising.

Shattering.

The breath left her on a small scream, shrill and desperate. She was on fire. Flying. Exploding into a million shards. She felt a hand cup her cheek, heard Chuckie's voice, low and harsh, but couldn't make out the words. And then his mouth was on hers, anchoring her in place as the fiery storm washed over her. His hold on her tightened as he drove into her, over and over, sending her deeper into the tempest. Then his own body tensed and stilled, his growl long and low as his own climax exploded between them. Taylor clung to him, swallowing each of his harsh breaths as time slowed around them.

He eased his mouth away from hers, sucked in a deep breath, then dropped his head against her shoulder. Minutes slipped by, filled with nothing more than the sound of their mingled breathing.

Chuckie finally raised his head, his deep blue gaze meeting hers. He pressed a quick kiss against the corner of her mouth then leaned back, a small grin teasing the edges of his mouth. "I'm not sure I can move after that."

Taylor tried to fight her own grin then gave up. "Me either."

"Good. We can just stay like this all night."

"I don't think that's going to work."

Chuckie rested his forehead against her shoulder and grunted. "Why not?"

"Because it's not very practical."

"Since when do you care about practical?"

"I don't." She turned her head and nipped his earlobe, smiling when a shudder went through him. "But I'm thinking the bed will be more comfortable."

Chuckie opened one eye and watched her, his gaze warming something deep inside her. "Is that an invitation?"

She almost asked for what, but stopped herself at the last minute. Yes, it was an invitation to the stay the night. But was it more than that? Is that what he was asking? Or was she reading too much into it? Taylor didn't think so, but now wasn't the time for that conversation—if they even needed to have that conversation.

So she simply smiled and nodded and did her best to ignore the way her heart fluttered in her chest when Chuckie smiled back.

chapter
FIFTEEN

Two hours until game time.

Charles slid closer to his desk, his fingers tapping a nervous beat on the only clean spot in front of him: the corner. And the only reason that small section was clear was because the coffee mug that usually sat there was currently in his other hand.

More coffee was the last thing he needed but that didn't stop him from taking a long swallow. One more wouldn't hurt, not with the way he was already bouncing around with nerves. And if he was this nervous, how was the team holding up?

He had watched from the window as cars slowly drifted in over the last thirty minutes. The coaching staff. A few of the players.

Taylor.

She had pulled her gear bag from the trunk of her car then paused and looked over her shoulder, glancing up at the window where he was standing. Could she see him? Yeah, obviously, because she gave him a quick smile and a short wave before slamming the trunk closed and walking across the parking lot.

He had watched her disappear inside before making his way back to his tiny cubicle and taking a seat at his desk. And he was still here, his mind a jumbled mess as he tried to ignore his jangling nerves.

Sex would probably be good for that. But it wasn't an option, not right now. And it hadn't been an option last night, either.

He had taken Taylor out to dinner last night, early. He shouldn't be feeling this hunger to see her again, not so soon. He told himself it was because they'd done nothing more than a quick goodnight kiss at her door—Taylor preferred to be by herself the night before a game, to take time to relax and do whatever it was she did to prepare. Charles told himself not to take it personally, reminded himself that lots of athletes had different rituals before each game.

Maybe he should come up with his own ritual, because sitting here overanalyzing everything—with Taylor, with the team, with the upcoming game—wasn't doing him or his nerves any good. He'd add that to his to-do list, right after everything else.

The door at the end of the hall opened and closed. Footsteps, steady and sure, moved closer. Charles didn't have to look to know who it was. Murphy was here, only a little later than expected.

The older man stopped in front of Charles' cubicle, looking every inch the professional businessman in an expensive designer suit. "Are we set for everything today?"

"Everything is good to go."

"Good. Good." Murphy glanced around the

cluttered cubicle then rested his steely gaze on Charles, no doubt sizing him up and making sure he was appropriately presentable. He was—or at least, he would be, as soon as he put on his tie.

"Run through the schedule again for me."

Charles placed the coffee mug back on the desk then grabbed the small planner spread open in front of the computer. "Channel 2 will be here an hour before the game for your interview. The reporter won't be staying, but they agreed to leave a film crew to capture some of the game. The Sun and the Times will both be here in time for the first face off. You have an interview scheduled for the first intermission and another one for the second intermission."

Murphy nodded his pleasure. "Good. Excellent. And after the game?"

"Channel 2 is promising to send a reporter back for that. Channel 13 says they'll try to get someone out but no guarantees. It's going to depend on what else happens."

"Then I guess we hope for a slow news day. What about Channel 11 or 45? Anything from them?"

"Nothing concrete, no." Charles watched the older man, studying his expression for any sign of irritation or disappointment. There was none. At least, none that Charles could see. Was that good or bad? Time would tell. Maybe.

Charles glanced back at the planner, running through the list with the tip of one blunt nail. "There are also two small newspapers—one from the county and one from the eastern shore—that are going to be here, as well as a reporter from the community college. I'm hoping to do a small press conference after the game but—" Charles let the words fade into the silence. There wouldn't be any sense in holding a press conference if there wasn't any press around. All he could do now was wait and see. And hope.

"I guess that'll do for now." Murphy reached up and smoothed the silk tie, then readjusted the cuffs of his shirt with a precise tug on each. "I'm going down to talk to the girls. Give them a little pep talk. Would you care to join me?"

Charles glanced at the clock hanging over his desk then turned back to Murphy with a frown. "Is now a good time? They're probably getting ready for the game and—"

"Nonsense. Of course, it's a good time. Why wouldn't it be?"

"It's just—" Charles hesitated, searching for the right words. "Sometimes athletes have rituals—I mean, routines—that they do to get ready. They might be busy—"

"I know all about that superstitious nonsense and that's exactly what it is: nonsense. I'm the owner. There's nothing wrong with me stopping in and giving them a pep talk."

"James, you have to remember these are women. It's probably not a good idea to just barge into the locker room and—"

"Are you coming with me or not?" Impatience flashed in the steel of Murphy's eyes. Charles bit back the rest of what he was going to say and nodded. "Good. Grab your tie and let's go."

Charles did just that, wrangling the silk around his neck as he followed the older man downstairs. The rink was still eerily deserted and oddly quiet as they walked through, heading toward the main locker room. He could hear voices, muted and muffled, as they approached. Not just from the main locker room, but from the visitor's room as well. Was it his imagination, or could he actually sense the nervous anticipation seething under the doors?

Or maybe that was his own nervous anticipation. Today was a big day—for all of them. And if he was feeling this nervous, he could only imagine how bad it was in each locker room.

Murphy stopped in front of the door and raised his hand, knocking against it twice. Then he pushed through without warning, entering the locker room with a hearty greeting. Charles winced as nineteen faces—players and coaching staff together—turned toward them, all of them wearing expressions ranging from astonishment to irritation. Two of the girls made small gasps of surprise and quickly turned away as they pulled shirts over their heads. One set of eyes found his, irritation flashing in their whiskey depths.

Heat flooded his face and he had to force himself not to rush over to Taylor and cover her with his jacket. She stood there, her chin tilted at a defiant angle, wearing nothing more than compression shorts, hockey socks, and a sports bra. A moisture-wicking shirt was held in one hand but she made no move to put it on. She also wasn't doing a very good job of hiding the anger flashing in her eyes.

"Mr. Murphy." Coach Reynolds's voice was short and clipped. Her hand tightened around the clipboard as she stepped closer, so close that James actually backed up a step. "Now isn't a good time—"

"Nonsense. I just came to tell the girls—"

"Again, this isn't a good time." Coach moved forward, each step forcing Murphy—and Charles—back toward the door. One more step and they were standing outside the locker room, the door swinging shut behind Coach Reynolds.

Anger flared in her eyes and colored her cheeks as she pointed a finger in Murphy's face. Charles held his breath, waiting to see what the man would do, but he simply stood there, his lined face comically blank.

"Don't you ever—and I mean *ever*—come into the locker room unannounced again. Is that clear? And never before a game. What the hell do you think you're doing?"

James blinked, color seeping into his face. A second went by, then another, before he squared his shoulders and leaned forward, meeting Coach's glare with his own.

"You're forgetting that I'm the owner. Those girls work for *me*. And so do you."

"I don't give a shit. Those ladies are mine, not yours, regardless of what you think. And I'm telling you right now, if you ever dare come into the locker room before a game again without being invited, there will be hell to pay. Is that understood?"

"Now see here—"

Coach stepped forward, shorter than James by a head but a thousand times more intimidating. "Is that understood?"

Silence stretched around them, tense and sharp. Charles remained perfectly still, afraid to draw the coach's attention even if he did happen to agree with her. He watched, waiting to see what Murphy would do, wondering if the Blades would suddenly be out a head coach in the next thirty seconds.

To his surprise, James finally nodded and stepped back, the anger that had colored his cheeks slowly fading. He nodded, just a curt motion of his head. "My apologies, Diane. It won't happen again."

"Good. Make sure it doesn't." She lowered her hand then glanced over at Charles, as if she was seeing him for the first time. She frowned then looked back at Murphy. "Now what is it you wanted?"

"I just wanted to wish the girls good luck, that was all."

"Fine. You can do that." She held up her hand, stopping Murphy before he could move, and looked at her watch. "In twenty minutes. I'll come out and get you. Will that work?"

Murphy's eyes narrowed, the first hint of impatience finally cracking his smooth veneer. But he didn't say anything, just simply nodded. Coach studied him for a few long seconds, almost as if she was waiting for him to say or do something. Then she spun on her heel and pushed through the locker room door without another word.

Charles stood there, uncertainty tugging at him. He briefly considered walking away, pretending he hadn't witnessed the verbal altercation. He was getting ready to do just that when James turned toward him, something that almost resembled a smile wreathing his face.

"She does have spirit, doesn't she?"

"Coach Reynolds? Um, yes. Yes, she does."

"And she's one hell of a coach, too. No doubt in my mind she's doing a great job with the girls." Murphy laughed, the sound loud in the rink. He clapped a hand on Charles' shoulder then motioned toward the offices. "Why don't we head back and make sure everything's ready? Then we can come back in twenty minutes."

"I don't think you need me—"

"Nonsense. You're the PR Director. I'm sure the

girls would like to hear an update before the game. Now, let's go back and you can tell me what else we're working on while we wait."

Charles bit back a groan of irritation and followed Murphy toward the office. But he wasn't listening to the older man.

He was remembering the anger that flashed in Taylor's eyes and the way her chin tilted in stubborn defiance. And he couldn't shake the feeling that it wasn't because of their unexpected entry into the locker room.

What the hell had happened to make her so angry?

Chapter SIXTEEN

Taylor jumped the boards with Rachel and Dani, her blades hitting the ice with a loud scratching noise as she took off toward the puck. The surface was rough, too rough, causing the puck to bounce and skip. For once, it bounced in their favor. She reached out with the blade of her stick and pulled the puck in close, spinning around and taking off across center ice. Dani pulled up beside her and tapped her stick against the gouged surface. Taylor glanced around, making sure Dani was still open, then shot the puck toward her and skated into position. A defenseman from Richmond moved behind her, crowding her, blocking any chance she might have of shooting if she got the puck back.

Taylor muttered under her breath and shifted left. Right. Left again, trying to shake the other woman. Damn. She was stuck to her like glue. Taylor spun around, her gaze landing on Rachel. She tapped her stick and called out, trying to get the other woman's attention. But Rachel wasn't paying any attention, at least not to Taylor. She wasn't even in position, not even close.

Anger and impatience rushed through her. Dammit. What the hell was Rachel's problem? She'd been out of position all afternoon, screwing up damn near every single play. As much as Taylor didn't care for her, this wasn't like the other woman. Or was it? Was Woodhouse still so angry that she'd deliberately screw up every scoring chance they got this afternoon?

The tension had come to a head in the locker room, minutes before Mr. Murphy had barged in. Rachel had been pissed when she learned she was playing third line. And of course her anger had been directed at Taylor, because somehow it was all Taylor's fault. They'd gotten up into each other's faces, had damn near come to blows before Coach Reynolds separated them—

And quietly told Taylor to handle it. She had tried—but it hadn't worked. Rachel had stormed off, shooting dirty looks her way as she huddled with Jordyn and Amanda, no doubt plotting some twisted revenge. Or maybe just wishing death and dismemberment on her.

To make matters worse, the team's play had gone to shit during the first period and Coach had changed the lines around, finally moving Rachel up with Taylor for a few plays.

And now it looked like Rachel was deliberately screwing up. But why? It made no sense.

Taylor ground her teeth together, feeling the mouthpiece give a little under the pressure. Screw it. She couldn't worry about Rachel right now, not when it meant risking a scoring chance. She tapped her stick on the ice, trying to get Dani's attention, then spun around and used her stick to push against the defenseman who kept getting in her way.

She managed to free herself and moved forward two feet when the whistle split the air. Taylor slid to a stop, glancing at the ref in surprise when he pointed at her and clenched both fists, moving them out straight out from his chest.

"Number 67. Two minutes. Cross-checking."

"What? No way." Taylor started to move closer but Sammie skated toward her, stopping her.

"Taylor, don't. You know better."

Taylor hesitated, her eyes narrowing at the official. She bit back the words of argument that wanted to fall from her mouth and headed toward the penalty box. Rachel moved closer, a sneer marring her smooth features.

"Way to go, LeBlanc. Way to screw us over."

"Fuck you. Maybe if you'd get your head in the game—"

Sammie grabbed her elbow and pulled her away, warning flashing in her brown eyes. Taylor nodded once then skated away, wondering what the hell was wrong with her. It wasn't just the penalty—that she could at least understand. Maybe she didn't agree with it. Maybe it was borderline. Maybe it was just a bad call. She could live with that. Mostly.

But to come close to getting into it with her own teammate, right there on the ice? That was inexcusable—even if it was Rachel Woodhouse. She knew better.

She stormed into the penalty box and dropped to the bench, her hands tightening around the stick as she watched the Blades move to the penalty kill. They were down by one point. If Richmond scored on the power play, it would be Taylor's fault.

Her eyes followed the puck down the ice and she held her breath, watching as Richmond shot once, twice. Once more. Shannon caught the puck on the last shot and pulled it into her chest as the whistle split the air, calling the play dead.

Taylor breathed a sigh a of relief then looked around at the scattering of applause coming from the crowd. Except maybe *crowd* was being too generous. There were a thousand seats in the arena, and less than half were filled.

Hardly a crowd.

Chuckie had told her they'd sold 576 tickets. More than half, even though it didn't look like it. Not bad for their very first game, especially since it was a Saturday afternoon and the Banners had their own opening game in a few hours. At least, that's what everyone kept saying. But Taylor couldn't quite hide the disappointment that filled her every time she looked around, and she knew her teammates felt the same way.

It would be worse if they lost.

They couldn't lose. They just couldn't.

Taylor adjusted the helmet on her face then got to her feet, her eyes moving from the play on the ice to the clock as it counted down the seconds.

Fifteen seconds. Richmond was cycling the puck, looking for an opening.

Ten seconds. They took a shot, only to have Shannon deflect it off to the side.

Five seconds. Another shot, this one wide. Sammie raced for the puck, cradled it against her stick, and looked over at Taylor.

Two seconds. One...

Taylor raced out of the penalty box as Sammie shot the puck toward her. She held her breath, praying it wouldn't bounce, praying it wouldn't skip—

The puck tapped the blade of her stick like a long-lost lover coming home. Taylor twirled and took off toward the net, hearing the shouts and swearing coming from the players behind her.

But they were too far behind her, with no chance of catching her. Richmond's goalie anticipated her move and dropped into position, her left leg dragging to the side as she slid to the right. Taylor stopped, spun around, then darted to the left and flipped the puck into the air. She held her breath, watching as the goalie stretched her arm out to the side, trying to catch it. The puck tipped off her glove and hit the back of the net.

The red light flashed as the horn sounded, signaling the Blades' first official goal. Taylor dropped to one knee and slid across the ice, pumping her fist in celebration as her teammates rushed toward her.

Taylor tapped the top of Sammie's helmet as they headed toward the bench. Coach Reynolds silently watched as Taylor climbed over the boards. She didn't say a word—she didn't have to. Yes, Taylor had scored, but it had been nothing more than perfect timing. It could have easily gone the other way, with Richmond capitalizing on the power play and putting the Blades down by two.

Because Taylor had screwed up and drawn the penalty.

She nodded at the coach, letting the woman know she understood. Then she dropped to the bench and reached for one of the water bottles, her gaze scanning the scattered faces of the crowd.

She found who she was looking for a few rows

behind the penalty box, where she knew they'd be. Her family: Mom and Dad, Mia and Cassie. Aunt Emily and Uncle JP and Tristan and the twins. Her mom and Aunt Emily were smiling and her sisters were both giving her the thumbs-up sign. But she saw the carefully blank expression on her father's face—and Uncle JP's as well. Yes, they were happy she scored. But there was no doubt she'd get a lecture from both of them later tonight or tomorrow at dinner.

Oh well. No more than she deserved.

She looked down the ice, her gaze searching for another familiar face. Chuckie was standing with Mr. Murphy and a group of people, a few of them with cameras. The press, such as it was. At least they looked happy. At least, she thought they did.

She took another swig of water then handed the bottle to Sammie before turning her attention back to the ice.

Yes, the Blades were finally on the board. But it was only the second period and they were tied with Richmond. A lot could happen in the next twenty-nine minutes.

They just needed to make sure it happened in their favor.

chapter
SEVENTEEN

"Guys! Enough. Be quiet here. I'm trying to make a damn toast!" Shannon brushed the long blonde hair away from her face with an impatient swipe of one hand and raised her glass of beer. She frowned, belched, then wobbled a little on the chair. Dani laughed and grabbed her leg, holding her steady so she wouldn't fall.

Taylor laughed with everyone else when Shannon swiped at Dani's hand then nearly fell. She let out a little screech that was totally uncharacteristic for her and grabbed the back of the chair, catching herself before she toppled to the floor.

"Oops. Okay. I'm not drunk. I swear." Shannon steadied herself then grinned as she looked around the table. "Not much, anyway."

More laughter erupted around them when Shannon frowned and stared into her glass. "What was I saying? Oh, yeah. Okay. A toast. To the best fucking hockey team around!"

Cheers went up and everyone reached for their drinks. Shannon took a long swallow of the beer, belched again, then raised her glass once more. "And to Jordyn, for the game-winning goal. Which was abso-fucking-lutely beautiful, by the way!"

More cheers and applause as everyone raised their glasses in Jordyn's direction. She smiled and shot a quick glance at Taylor. "Yeah, well. It was a beautiful set-up."

Taylor simply nodded, too stunned to do more than that. Had Jordyn actually complimented her? Maybe she was reading too much into it. Or maybe it was just the alcohol talking. Yeah, that had to be it.

They'd been at The Ale House—a casual sports bar and nightclub in Timonium—for two hours already, celebrating their first win of the season. It hadn't been an easy one, and it certainly hadn't been pretty, either. But they'd won just the same, thanks to Jordyn's hard shot in the last minute of the game.

They had come here to celebrate, after the coaching staff had said their spiel in the locker room. Yes, they'd won. Yes, they had reason to celebrate. But they still had plenty to work on—*all* of them.

Taylor hadn't missed the way Coach Reynolds had looked at her and Rachel when she'd said that last part. And Taylor knew she had screwed up, had owned up to it. But she didn't want to dwell on that now. She wanted to celebrate, just like everyone else.

Sammie nudged her leg under the table then leaned in, her voice lowered so only Taylor could hear it. "Holy crappola. Did Jordyn Knott just give you compliment?"

"I think. Talk about miracles, huh?"

"Yup." Sammie nodded, the mop of dark curls bouncing around her face with the motion. She blew one stray curl out of her eyes and glanced around the table. "Too bad Woodhouse wants to kill you, though."

Taylor followed Sammie's gaze, swallowing back a sigh of frustration along with a hefty swig of beer. Rachel sat at the far end of the table, a scowl permanently etched on her face. She hadn't played for the last fifteen minutes of the game, and Taylor had no doubt that she was getting the blame for it.

Part of her was tempted to go over and talk to the other woman. To just...something. Clear the air. Ask her what her problem was. Have it out, once and for all.

Taylor sighed and leaned back in the chair. Talking to Rachel wouldn't help. Not here. Not now, when the other woman was still so obviously pissed off. It wouldn't be a talk, it would be an argument. Probably a loud one. Now wasn't the time for it.

The only problem was, Taylor wasn't sure there would ever be a time for it.

A bout of laughter caught her attention and she turned toward the noise, just in time to see Shannon try to jump from the chair. The move lacked her normal grace and coordination and she stumbled, hitting the edge of the table and nearly upending it. Glasses and bottles clanked as they slid, only to be caught at the last minute by several mad grabs.

"Oopsie shitty." Shannon dropped into her chair with a laugh then stared straight ahead, unblinking for a few long seconds.

Karly Durant, their backup goalie, leaned forward, a crooked smile on her face. "Somebody cut her off before she gets us thrown out."

Shannon grabbed her glass before Dani could take it, holding it close to her chest. "Hey. No. I'm good. I was just thinking."

"Oh shit. That's never good."

"No. Serious." Shannon's expression cleared and she turned toward Karly. "What did you say the number was?"

"What number?"

"People. You know—" Shannon waved her hand around, her fingers wiggling in the air. "People. Watchers. Um—"

"Spectators?" Karly helpfully supplied the word.

"Yeah. That's it. What was the number?"

"Three hundred and ninety-two."

Silence settled around the table for a few long minutes, broken only when Shannon let out a long sigh. "God. That's fucking depressing."

Taylor looked over with a frown. "Are you sure that's right?"

"Yup. I counted. Three times."

"No, that can't be right."

"Wish it wasn't but it is."

"But they sold 576 tickets. Are you sure you didn't miscount?"

"Yup. Positive." Karly tossed back the rest of her soda and put the glass back down with a heavy *thud*, the sound oddly loud in the silence that surrounded their table.

Sammie broke the silence with a soft question, her voice filled with the disappointment that was clear on everyone's faces. "That's probably not a good thing, is it?"

"I don't know. Maybe. Probably not." Taylor raised her glass then changed her mind and sat it back down. "I mean, it was the first game, right? Nobody can judge the attendance on just one game. I don't think."

"Do they go by ticket sales or actual bodies?"

"I have no idea. Ticket sales, I hope. I mean, the tickets are already paid for, right? That means they have the money. Isn't that what counts?"

"That's probably the only thing Mr. Murphy cares about, anyway." Heads nodded at Dani's words, most of the players in agreement—Taylor included. None of them had a good feel for the owner yet, although the general consensus was that he didn't have a clue about the sport—or the players.

Karly leaned forward, her gaze catching Taylor's. "How do you know how many tickets they sold?"

"Chuckie told me."

Several heads turned in her direction, with expressions ranging from surprise and curiosity to outright gleaming calculation—the last one coming from Rachel. Taylor turned away from the woman's narrowed glare, trying to ignore the odd shiver the look sent through her.

"When he did he tell you that?"

"Yeah. And *why* would he tell you?" Amanda leaned forward, expectation and something more than simple curiosity on her face.

Sammie nudged Taylor's leg under the table then pasted a bright smile on her face. "He told me, too. Last Saturday after practice."

Taylor knew the exact minute Rachel realized Sammie was lying—she saw it in the way her eyes narrowed and her lips pursed, in the spark of interest that flashed across her face. Rachel and Taylor had been the last ones at practice Saturday, because Coach had made them stay late to do laps. Rachel *knew* Sammie wasn't there—but Sammie didn't know that.

Taylor made a big show of laughing and nudged Sammie in the side. "You've got your days mixed up. It wasn't Saturday. It was Tuesday."

"It was? Oh. Yeah. Um. Tuesday. Sure." Sammie laughed and tilted her head from side to side like a little kid. "Silly me. You know how confused I get. Always mixing up days and—"

Taylor kicked her under the table before she could say anything else. Sammie's mouth snapped shut and she reached for the glass of wine she had been sipping all night.

"Who cares when he told you. What I want to know is, what are they going to worry about more: the sales, or the bodies?"

Shannon reached across the table for the pitcher of beer and refilled her glass. "Why are we even worrying about this? There's nothing we can do about it and it's too freaking depressing anyway. Let's talk about something else. Like Chuckie's fine ass. That man is certainly sweet on the eyes."

Laughter erupted around the table, dissipating the odd tension that had been hovering over it seconds earlier. Taylor shot the goalie a warning glance, wondering why in the hell Shannon had taken the conversation in that direction. She certainly didn't feel like listening to everyone talk about Chuckie, especially not like that. And not with the way Rachel was suddenly paying close attention to every word.

Sammie must have picked up on her discomfort because she leaned forward, catching Jordyn's attention. "So how did the interview go after the game? Did they ask you any stupid questions?"

"No, not really. I mean, a few of them were kind of stupid but it was mostly good. I guess." Jordyn looked around the table and shrugged. "I've never done an interview before so I'm not sure. Not like it matters, anyway."

"How can you say that? Of course, it matters."

"No, it doesn't. It probably won't even air. Face it—nobody cares about the league or the team."

Silence fell over the table once more, its weight oppressive and smothering. Shannon swore, loud, then pushed away from the table.

"God, this is such bullshit, guys. Come on, we need to stop. We're supposed to be celebrating, right? No more game talk. It is what it is for right now, and there's nothing we can do about it. So let's go celebrate."

Dani reached up and tugged on her arm. "Hey, genius. We *are* celebrating. Sit down before you get us thrown out or something."

"This isn't a celebration. And we're not going to get thrown out. We need to do something besides sit here. We won, guys! Our first game. That's something to be proud of." Shannon leaned down and grabbed Dani, pulling her to her feet. Then she hurried around the table, grabbing one player after another until everyone was standing—everyone except Rachel and Amanda, who were too busy whispering to each other.

"Wiley, why are we all standing around here?"

"Because we're not standing. We're walking. Come on, let's go. One foot after another—"

"Walking where?"

Shannon pointed to the door leading to the nightclub side. "Right through there. And then we're all going to have a few more drinks and dance until we forget all this depressing bullshit."

"Shannon, it's too early. There's probably nobody over there."

"That just means we'll have the place to ourselves. Come on, guys, get moving."

A soft mix of laughter and groans greeted her commands, yet everyone started moving toward the nightclub. Taylor glanced over her shoulder, not surprised to see Rachel and Amanda still sitting there, deep in heavy conversation, their gazes darting to hers and quickly moving away. Her stomach started to knot as she wondered what they were talking about, then she realized she didn't care.

"Just ignore them. It's not worth worrying about."

Taylor spun around, surprised to see Jordyn standing there. She was even more surprised at her words. Jordyn pushed the dark hair out of her face, the corner of her mouth tilting in something close to a smile. "Rachel's dealing with some...stuff. You know?"

"No, not really. And what does that have to do with me?"

"Nothing, except she needs someone to take it out on."

"Lucky me."

"Yeah, well. It doesn't help that she's jealous of you. And that she doesn't like you."

"Wow. Really? I couldn't tell."

Another small smile lifted the corners of Jordyn's mouth, there and gone in the blink of an eye. She glanced around then turned back to Taylor and leaned closer, her voice lowered.

"I just wanted to say thanks. For feeding me that shot earlier. I know you didn't have to."

Taylor frowned, not bothering to hide her

bewilderment. "Why wouldn't I? You were in perfect position."

"Not really. You could have just as easily made that shot. We both know it."

"No. I was too far away. You had the better chance."

Jordyn watched her for a long second, her gray eyes serious and focused. She glanced over at Rachel and Amanda then turned back to Taylor. "Not everyone would have done that, and we both know it. So, thanks."

Taylor stood there, stunned, as Jordyn walked away. She hadn't expected that—any of it—and she wondered what was behind it. If there was a reason Jordyn had approached her. Maybe she actually meant the words, maybe she didn't. Did it matter?

Not really. Taylor hoped that it meant they'd at least be on friendly terms, but she wasn't going to hold her breath—not after all the friction and tension that had been between them the last few months.

Sammie stepped closer, her gaze on Jordyn as the other woman headed into the nightclub. "What was that all about?"

"Honestly? I have no idea. But I'm hoping it was a step in the right direction."

"Hm. Maybe. But I wouldn't really trust her just yet." Sammie stared at something behind Taylor and frowned. "And I sure as anything wouldn't trust those two."

She glanced over her shoulder, her gaze meeting Rachel's for several long seconds. She tried to ignore the anger and hatred that flared in the other woman's eyes, tried to tell herself it didn't matter. But it did, and she wasn't sure why.

Taylor turned back around with a sigh and followed Sammie across the floor. "Trust me. I don't."

chapter
EIGHTEEN

Charles hung up the phone then leaned back in the chair, disappointment threatening to cloud his vision. He wanted to scream. To kick something. To curl his hand into a fist and put it through a wall.

He closed his eyes and took a deep breath instead, slowly releasing it through his clenched teeth. This was nothing more than one more disappointment in a long line of disappointments. Just another obstacle. He should be used to it by now, right?

Hell, he had told himself he wanted the challenge, that he was up for it. Nothing like a nice challenge to sharpen his skills and focus his mind.

But fuck, it would be nice to catch one break. Just one. Was that asking for too much?

Apparently.

He glanced at his watch and bit back a curse. The meeting was starting in five minutes and he had absolutely nothing new to report. There was no more interest now than there had been since the first game three weeks ago. And the Blades had won all three—their first two at home, as well as their road game in New York on Saturday.

It didn't matter that the other teams were hitting the same brick wall he was: a complete lack of interest in women's hockey. It made no sense. He hadn't expected news outlets to be beating down his door with requests, but he hadn't expected this depressing wall of silence, either. Would this weekend's little exhibition at the Banners' home game help? Maybe. But he couldn't count on it.

And with a very limited budget for advertising, he was trapped. Social media only worked for so long. Low-budget ads in the local papers only reached so far. And forget television spots—there simply wasn't enough money for that.

Hell, the team barely had enough money to fix the fucking ice, something the girls had complained about—loudly—after their first game. He'd gone out there himself and could see exactly what they were talking about. And if he could see it, with his limited experience, why the hell couldn't Murphy?

Because Murphy wasn't looking at it the same way. Not even close. To Murphy and the rest of his cronies, this was nothing more than a quaint experience. A chance to live out a dream of owning a sports team. If it didn't work out, it would be nothing more than a tax write-off for the older man.

But it was a hell of a lot more than that to the ladies. To Taylor. Why couldn't Murph see that? It wasn't Charles's job, not even close, but even he could see something needed to change. If it didn't, Taylor's fears would become a reality: everything would implode before the season was halfway over.

Charles pushed back his anger and grabbed the thick file from the corner of his desk. He wasn't looking forward to the meeting, wasn't looking forward to dropping some cold hard truths on the table. It needed to be done, though, and he wasn't sure there was anyone else who could do it.

He pushed through the doors of the conference room, his gaze sweeping across the expensive leather chairs and gleaming surface of the custom table. Anger flashed through him again but he pushed it down, holding it in check as James turned toward him.

"Chuck. I was just getting ready to call you. What have you got for us? Good news, I hope. Ticket sales aren't even close to what we were hoping for."

Charles opened his mouth then quickly snapped it closed. His carefully planned speech hovered right on the tip of his tongue, but he couldn't get the words out. Six sets of eyes watched him, their bored faces filled with nothing more than polite patience. Only Murphy looked like he was remotely interested, but not for the right reasons.

Not even close.

Charles scanned each impassive face, taking in the expensive designer suits and flashy rings and watches. His gaze rested on the large, intricately-cut Waterford crystal bowl that sat in the middle of the polished table then traveled to the new, state-of-the-art AV system built into the far wall. Why the hell did they even need it? Nobody was using it as far as he knew, not even the coaching staff, who filmed the practices and games on someone's personal camera then watched them at home.

Charles tossed the overstuffed file onto the table,

hard enough that papers scattered across the surface. He leaned forward and planted his fists on the table then fixed Murphy with a frigid glare.

"How much was this table?"

Thick white brows shot up above steely eyes. "Chuck, I don't think—"

"How about this bowl? How much? A couple grand?" Charles pushed away from the table and moved to the end of the room, all eyes focused on him as he stopped in front of the AV system. "Or this? How much?"

"I don't see—"

"When the hell has anyone ever used it, Murph?" He pulled in a deep breath and let it out, slow and even as he walked around the table. Murph was staring at him, surprise and anger simmering in his steely eyes. Had Charles expected anything different? No, of course not. Not really. Hell, he didn't know what he expected.

So he might as well keep going.

"You've spared no expense when it comes to this front office. It was designed to impress and it sure as hell does its job. The only problem is, nobody is interested in coming here. Local media is less-than-enthusiastic about the entire team. The majority of the public doesn't even know the Blades exist. And those that do know don't care enough. There's nothing to entice them into coming. Nothing—"

"That's exactly why we brought you on, Chuck. It's your job to get them here."

His temper flared and he leaned across the table again. "With what? You gave me a job to do but absolutely no budget to work with. You sit up here in your designer suits surrounded by all the trimmings that scream success while downstairs, the girls are risking broken ankles by playing on destroyed ice. And they're doing it for damn near free."

"That's not true. They get paid. All of them."

Charles laughed, the sound sharp and bitter. "Paid? You can actually sit there and say that with a straight face? Every single one of them works another job. Some of them are working two jobs. But they keep showing up here, busting their asses, because they love the game."

"And where exactly do you suggest we pull money from? Ticket sales are stagnant. Like you said, people aren't interested. That was your job, Chuck. To get them interested."

Charles didn't miss the man's use of the past-tense. Had he just shot himself in the foot? Maybe. What the hell. He might as well keep going. It certainly couldn't hurt.

"You need to increase the marketing budget. Let me run some real ads. Come up with some giveaways and incentives to get people through the door. Look into sponsors. Spend some money for a line of souvenirs to offer for sale. Hell, something. *Anything.* Get the damn ice fixed before someone gets hurt. And do something about that damn bus you've got the team using for their road games. It has an exhaust leak that's damn near deadly."

Silence, thick and heavy, settled over the room. A few of the men dropped their gazes, focusing on the table. One or two looked out the large tinted window. But not Murphy.

The older man watched him with those steely eyes, his jaw set and his back and shoulders rigid. Charles met that cold look. Refusing to look away, refusing to back down.

He expected Murph to tell him to get lost. To tell him to clean out his desk and start looking for a new job. Fair enough—Charles knew that was a possibility before he opened his mouth. It would suck, but he could find another job. Because he was that good.

At least, he was that good when he actually had something to work with.

Murph finally broke eye contact and glanced around the table. He frowned then turned back to Charles. "How do you know all this?"

"Know all what?"

"About the ice. The bus. The girls working other jobs. How do you know?"

Christ, was he serious? Yes, he was. Charles ran a hand through his hair and shook his head. "Because I talk to them, Murph. Because I've gotten to know them. Maybe you should try it."

And yeah, that time he had gone too far. He could see it in the way color blossomed on Murph's face and in the way the older man's eyes narrowed. The man next to Murph—Charles couldn't remember his name—leaned in and said something in a low voice. Murph frowned again, shot another dangerous look at Charles, then turned back to the other man, still listening to whatever was being said. A long minute went by, filled with thick tension.

Murphy released a loud sigh, sat back in the chair, and steepled his fingers under his chin. The silence continued to stretch around them, long enough that Charles actually shifted his weight from one foot to the other, feeling like a kid ready to receive some kind of harsh punishment.

"I'll make sure money is added to your budget.

And I'll have someone look into the bus situation. Will that work?"

Charles blinked, wondering if he was hearing things. No, he wasn't. It took more control than he thought it would to keep his mouth from dropping open in shock. "Yeah. Yes. That would be great."

"Good. Now, about the other things." Murphy glanced at the man next to him then turned back to Charles. "A few of us will be at practice tomorrow night. Make sure you're there. I want you to introduce the girls to everyone. And then I want you to have someone show me what the problem is with the ice."

"Yes, of course. No problem."

"Good." Murph pushed away from the table and stood, a clear signal of dismissal. Charles reached for the scattered papers and shoved them back into the folder, ready to disappear before Murphy changed his mind.

"Chuck? One more thing."

"Yeah?"

"I'm still expecting results. And soon. Understood?"

"Yeah. Absolutely." Charles nodded, glanced around the room and nodded again, then hurried out.

Holy shit. It had worked. Not that he had been planning on saying any of that, but it had worked. It was a start.

He glanced at his watch, wondering if it was too early to call Taylor. She was working at the gym until five tonight but her job was pretty flexible. Did she have a client right now? He couldn't remember.

It didn't matter. He'd still call her. If she couldn't talk, he'd leave her a voicemail and give her the news. Maybe she'd even have some ideas on what to say and do tomorrow night because he sure as hell didn't.

chapter
NINETEEN

"This wasn't exactly what I had in mind, Tay-Tay."

"But it's brilliant. Come on, even you have to admit it."

Charles shook his head then leaned against the boards, damn near falling on his ass in the process. He ignored Taylor's small laugh and regained his balance, using the stick almost like a crutch. The only consolation was that he wasn't the only one having trouble staying upright on the ice.

"It's not going to be so brilliant if Murph keels over from a heart attack. It's never a good idea to kill the man with the money" He glanced at Taylor, something warm spreading through his chest at the sight of her small smile. She looked so natural, standing there on the ice, the skates nothing more than a natural extension of her body. Her thick hair was pulled back in a ponytail, the lights from above dancing on the light brown and honey blonde strands each time she moved.

She was wearing warm-up pants—probably over a pair of sweatpants, judging from the slight bulk—and an old green jersey free of any designs or logos. She held the stick in her gloved hands in front of her, her grip relaxed and casual.

She belonged on the ice, more than anyone else he'd ever seen. That didn't stop the urge he had to throw her over his shoulder and carry her off the ice. He almost laughed when he imagined her reaction. Yeah, he wouldn't get very far, not after she slugged him and dropped him on his ass.

"Mr. Murphy really isn't doing that bad."

Charles forced himself to focus on the here-and-now and looked over, his eyes automatically finding the owner of the Blades. He was at center ice, his ankles wobbling and his feet shuffling under him as he made slow progress along the ice. Sammie stood just in front of him, gliding backward, her arms held slightly in front of her—like she'd actually catch him if he fell.

"Do you really think pairing him with Sammie was a good idea? He'll crush her if he falls on top of her."

"Don't underestimate her size. She plays defense, remember? She can handle it. Besides, everyone loves Sammie. She's perfect for what's going to happen."

Charles turned his head to the side so fast, he nearly fell again. He ignored Taylor's outstretched arm and frowned, a sense of foreboding rushing through him. "What do you mean, for what's going to happen? Taylor, what the hell are you cooking up?"

"Relax. I'm not cooking up anything. You wanted him to get to know some of the team, right?"

"Yeah."

"Well, like I said, everyone loves Sammie. I mean, look at her. Those big brown eyes and that dark mop of curls. The way she's always smiling. She teaches kindergarten, for crying out loud."

"What does that have to do with anything?"

"Well, just look. Mr. Murphy is already entranced by her. See the way he's watching her, like he'd do anything to keep her safe?"

Charles looked closer, convinced Taylor was seeing things. Well, okay, maybe the older man *did* look like he could turn into a protective guard dog at any minute. Maybe—if Charles squinted his eyes and tilted his head to the side then looked really, really hard.

He shook his head and turned back to Taylor. "No, not really."

"You have no imagination, Chuckie." She laughed and tapped him on the leg with the bade of her stick, then used it to point. "Trust me on this, okay? And when Sammie starts telling him her story, he's going to go all soft and gooey and be willing to do anything for her."

"Her story?"

"Yeah. About how she fell so hard in love and got married and had Clare and thought it would be forever. Except then her jerk husband shipped out and served her with divorce papers from overseas with no warning. The dumb fuck."

"Uh, I don't think—"

Taylor cleared her throat and placed the blade of her stick back on the ice. "She's not going to say it quite like *that*."

"I hope not. But I don't think making up a story is going to help."

Taylor turned to face him, something sharp and cold flashing in her whiskey-colored eyes. "It's not a story. He really did divorce her. She packed up her few belongings and came back here to move in with her parents. I thought you knew that."

"No. I mean, I knew she was a single mom but I didn't know the rest of it." Charles looked over at the petite woman, sympathy welling inside him. He noticed that Murph suddenly looked sympathetic as well—sympathetic *and* troubled. Sammie shrugged and wiped a sleeve across her face as a wobbly smile lifted the corners of her mouth. Then her arms shot out to the side and started pinwheeling a second before she fell sideways on the ice.

Murph's eyes widened in surprise and he reached for the woman, doing his best to help her up. Sammie struggled to stand, her right foot wobbling and sliding out from under her.

"Oh shit. She's not hurt, is she?"

Taylor dropped one hand on his arm, holding him in place before he could start forward. "Just watch."

Sammie's foot slid out from under her one last time. She reached up, her hand catching Murph's, pulling him off-balance as well. The older man fell to his knees, an expression of astonishment crossing his face. Sammie spun around and curled her legs under her, then leaned forward, pointing to something on the ice. Murph frowned and leaned closer, then reached out with one hand and traced whatever it was Sammie was showing him.

"She's showing him one of the gouges we have to deal with. Telling him how dangerous it is and how the players have to be so careful and everything because they're so hazardous."

"Damn. You guys staged that?"

"Yup." Taylor's eyes sparkled with amusement. "Sammie's the best at embellishment. Told you this was brilliant."

"I'm impressed, Tay-Tay. This might actually work."

"Yeah? How impressed?"

He didn't miss the flash of heated excitement in her eyes, or the way her gaze dropped to his mouth for a fleeting second. An answering heat shot through him, his reaction going from zero to a hundred in a millisecond. And shit, now was *not* the time. Or the place.

That didn't stop him from leaning forward, his voice low as he spoke. "Impressed enough to do whatever you want."

"Yeah?" Taylor leaned closer too, her own voice heated and husky. "*Whatever* I want? I'm sure I can come up with something. Tonight."

Charles started to answer but Taylor jerked back, her eyes narrowing as she looked at something behind him. He frowned and followed her gaze, surprised to see Rachel Woodhouse and Amanda Beall watching them from their spot near the net. Neither woman looked happy, but there was something especially chilling about the expression on Rachel's face.

He turned back to Taylor. "What's that all about?"

"Who knows?"

"You sure about that?"

"As sure as I'll ever be."

"I take it things haven't gotten any better between the two of you?"

"Gee, you think?"

"You ever going to tell me what's going on?"

"Probably not."

"Taylor—"

"Not because I don't want to. Because I don't

know." She looked back over at the two women, her frown deepening, then turned back to him. "Honest, Chuckie. I really don't."

"She hasn't said anything—"

"No. And I don't feel like talking about it right now." She started to skate away then stopped and spun around, her ponytail whipping behind her as another smile warmed her face. "I almost forgot. Did you want to go to dinner Sunday after the game?"

"Yeah, sure. Was there any place you had in mind?"

A small flush stained her cheeks and she glanced away, suddenly shy. Her chest rose and fell with a deep breath then her gaze shot back to his. "Yeah. My parents. For Sunday dinner."

She spun around again and took off down the ice, leaving him standing there against the boards in stunned silence. Her parents? She wanted him to meet her family? He stood there for a long minute, wondering what the sensation was that was twisting his gut. Nerves? Yeah, definitely. But there was more to it than just nerves. Was he reading into it? Putting more importance on the invitation than there really was?

Did he *want* there to be more to it than simply having dinner at her parents' house? He didn't know. And part of him was afraid to look too closely at it—because what if he did, only to be wrong about it?

And shit, would he ever get rid of the last threads of self-doubt that seemed to follow him from his childhood? He thought he had, years ago—until he saw Taylor again. He needed to stop reading into things. Needed to stop overanalyzing and worrying and just enjoy things as they happened.

Sunday dinner with her parents. Not a big deal. He

could handle that. And there was no need to worry about it beforehand, not when there were a million other things to worry about.

Like the small exhibition at the Banners' game on Saturday night.

And making sure that Murphy and his cronies were suitably impressed with tonight. *That* was the biggest thing he needed to worry about right now.

Charles sucked in a deep breath and pushed away from the boards, heading toward Murphy at center ice and hoping for the best.

chapter TWENTY

"Holy crappola. Now *this* is what I call a locker room." Sammie dropped her bag on the bench and looked around, her eyes wide with amazement. The other girls were doing the same, a reverent hush hovering over the room as they filed in.

Taylor stopped next to Sammie and stared at the gear hanging in the open cubby. Pads. Helmet. Skates. Jerseys. This had to be Chuckie's doing. How else could their things have been placed here ahead of time?

Like they were professional hockey players, everything taken care of for them so they could focus on the game.

Except this wasn't a game—it was a quick, ten-minute show during the first intermission of the Banners' game tonight versus Tampa. They'd perform their little dog-and-pony show then come back here, get rid of their gear, put on clean jerseys, and be herded out to the concourse for autographs.

Please, let people show up for autographs.

Taylor pushed the negative thoughts from her mind and took a seat on the bench, trying to calm her racing nerves. It was stupid to have nerves. This wasn't a game. It meant nothing. In the grand scheme of things, it was nothing more than a tiny little inconsequential blip.

Except it wasn't. She didn't know why, but she was positive something big could come of tonight.

Or maybe it was just more wishful thinking on her part. A chance—just a tiny one—to play on the big ice. To pretend she was in the pros, like she'd always dreamed about.

Focus. Just stop and focus.

She kept repeating the words to herself as she pulled the gear from the cubby and stripped down so she could start dressing. Compression shorts. Pads. Hockey socks. Tape. Padded hockey shorts. Arm and chest pads. More tape. Her lucky moisture-wicking t-shirt emblazoned with the Banners' logo, the eagle and crossed hockey sticks faded with age. Sonny had given her two of them right before she played in the biggest game of her career not quite five years ago and brought home the gold.

She paused, sadness filling her at the memory. Almost five years? Had it really been that long ago? Yes, it had. She'd had such high hopes back then. Such big dreams. She'd been certain she'd be playing in the pros by now. Certain there would be a pro team for her to play on.

And there was. Kind of. If you put a really big positive spin on it. Just not the pros she had dreamed about.

She pushed the depressing thoughts away, telling

herself she was being melodramatic. That she was overreacting. No, things hadn't turned out like she had dreamed, but it could be worse—she could not be playing at all.

Taylor shoved her feet into the skates, tapping each one against the rubber mat covering the floor, then leaned down and started tying them. Tight and snug, the knots secure and tucked away. Then she folded her hands and let them hang between her legs, her eyes focused on the toes of her skates as she took a deep breath in and held it out for the count of five before releasing and repeating. Two more times, followed by one more, then she sat up and turned toward Sammie, ready to give her a high five. But Sammie wasn't looking at her—she was staring at the floor, one skate held in her hand, her face pale.

"Hey." Taylor nudged her in the side. "Are you okay?"

"I think I'm going to be sick."

"What? Why?" Taylor glanced around, looking for a trashcan or a bucket or something. "Are you coming down with something?"

"Yeah. Nerves. Holy crappola. I don't think I can do this."

"Yes, you can. We're just going out there to skate around. It's not even a game."

"What if they boo us? I don't think I could handle that."

"They're not going to boo us."

"Or what if everyone gets up to leave? That would be worse, I think."

Taylor thought about lying then changed her mind. "Well, some people will leave, sure. They'll want to go grab some food and beer and stuff or use the bathroom. But not everyone."

"I don't think that makes me feel any better."

"It'll be fine. Come on, finish getting ready."

Sammie tilted her head to the side and studied her with wide eyes. "How can you be so calm?"

"Who said I'm calm?"

"Well, if you're not, you're doing a great job of hiding it."

"Am I nervous? Yeah, a little. But that's normal."

"Easy for you to say. You've done this before."

Taylor tried to swallow her laughter, afraid it would come out sounding bitter. To her surprise, it wasn't. "Not since I was playing youth hockey and our team came here for the same thing. And that's been something like, I don't know—ten years, at least. Probably a little longer than that. Maybe twelve."

"Yeah, but you've still done it. I haven't. Not even anything close."

Taylor nudged her again. "Doesn't matter. Now come on, finish getting ready or you're going to miss the whole thing. What's Clare going to think if she doesn't see her mom out there tonight?"

Sammie pursed her lips then nodded, some color finally seeping into her face. "You're right. I can do this. No more nerves. I can't disappoint Clare."

Taylor laughed again then looked around the locker room. Everyone else was geared up and ready to go, sitting or standing in small groups, waiting to be told what to do next. Coach Reynolds pushed through the door, her focused gaze sweeping the room. She gave everyone a short nod and a quick smile.

"Remember ladies, this is just for fun. No pressure. A quick scrimmage, show off some of your moves, and then it's off the ice and back here to change before heading up to the concourse. I don't want anyone getting physical—save that for the game tomorrow. Any questions?"

There was a quick chorus of *no's* then Coach Reynolds read off the line-ups. Taylor bit back her surprise when she realized Rachel's and Amanda's names hadn't been called. She looked over, not surprised to see Rachel scowling in her direction.

Sammie leaned over, her voice pitched low as she whispered in Taylor's ear. "What's up with that?"

Taylor shook her head but didn't answer—not that she could, because she didn't have an answer.

Coach gave a short whistle and told everyone to line up. Then they were marching out of the room and down the hall, toward the ice. She could *smell* the ice, that tang of frozen air that tickled her nose. She could hear the scrape of blades against the frozen surface, hear the grunts and yells, the cheers of a crowd of thousands, the noise far away yet somehow amplified by the concrete walls of the hall.

Taylor's heart raced, fluttering with excitement beneath her breastbone. The feeling, so unexpected, caused her to stumble. Who had she been kidding, trying to tell herself this was no big deal? Maybe it wasn't a game, but it was still a big deal. A small taste of what she'd dreamed about her entire life.

The sound of a horn, its blare long and loud, split the chilled air as the crowd screamed. She didn't know what the score was, had no way of knowing, but the Banners were obviously winning. The crowd wouldn't be so wild if they weren't.

Sammie crowded closer and grabbed Taylor's arm, her head dropping against her back. "I think I'm going to be sick."

"Deep breaths, Reigler. Deep breaths. We've got this." Taylor took her own deep breaths, trying to calm the excitement racing through her.

Players from the Banners pushed their way through the hall, looming larger than life as they moved past. Taylor suddenly felt like she was ten years old again, small and insignificant compared to the giants she had looked up to when she was a kid. A memory floated to the surface, long-forgotten yet oh-so-poignant.

She had been standing in this same hallway, the stick held loose in her gloved hand, watching the players move past her. More than a few stopped to tap her on the head with their sticks, wishing her luck before heading back to the locker room.

Uncle JP knelt beside her, his knuckles rapping her helmet twice.

"Show them what you're made of, ma lutine. Remember the moves I showed you, eh?"

She grinned and bumped his fist. "You know it, John-Peere."

JP laughed at the nickname then moved past her, tapping the other kids on the head and wishing them luck as he moved by. Then Sonny was there, looming larger than life, such an intimidating man with the scar running down his cheek. Her new father, even though she hadn't started calling him Dad *yet.*

"All set, Pumpkin?"

"Yup."

"Not nervous?"

"No." She saw the way his brows shot up in surprise and quickly looked away. "Well, maybe a little."

"Nothing wrong with that. It keeps you sharp. Now go out there and have some fun. I'm proud of you, Pumpkin." He leaned down and pressed a quick kiss against the top of her

helmet then moved away, barking words of encouragement to her teammates as he passed by. She turned to watch him go, noticed Chuckie-the-fart standing beside her, an odd look on his face, one of anger and longing.

"You think you're so special, don't you Tay-Tay? Just because your father's some hot shot coach. Well, you're not special at all. He's not even your real father."

"Shut up, Chuckie. You don't know what you're talking about. And at least I have a father, you stupid—"

Their coach had come up to separate them before she could say anything else, and then it was time for them to go onto the ice, to play in front of thousands of people.

Taylor blinked, the memory fading as quickly as it had appeared. She blinked again, surprised at the burning sensation in her eyes, surprised at the moisture filling them. She reached up and rubbed her chest with one gloved hand, surprised it was so tight. God, she hadn't thought about that day in…she wasn't sure how long. She remembered it, of course, but had never recalled the details until just now. Had she really been such a cocky little shit? Yes, she had. And Chuckie, the things she'd said to him—did he remember? He must have. How could he not remember?

Taylor blinked again and looked around, surprised to see Chuckie standing across from her, next to Coach Reynolds and Mr. Murphy. His ocean blue gaze was focused on her, filled with things she couldn't decipher. He smiled, one of his charming crooked ones, and stepped toward her, looking so dangerously masculine in the dark suit he wore. So different from the lonely boy she had so mercilessly teased all those years ago.

He tapped her on the helmet and dipped his head toward hers, his voice low and husky. "You think you're so special, don't you, Tay-Tay? Just because your father's some hot shot coach."

Taylor's eyes widened in surprise, her face heating in embarrassment. "You remember?"

Chuckie's grin widened and he leaned even closer. "Well, you are. You're more special than you realize."

Her heart slammed into her chest, making it hard to breathe. Sammie knocked into her from behind, freeing her from the odd paralysis caused by Chuckie's words. She sucked in a wheezing breath and stared at him, her eyes wide. "That's not what you said. Back then, I mean."

"I didn't know any better back then."

"Chuckie—"

He stepped back with a quick nod. "You better get going. They're going to start without you."

Taylor stumbled, helped by Sammie's quick nudge, then regained her balance and moved forward into the tunnel.

"Girl, you are so going to tell me what that was all about because wow, I'm having hot flashes like you wouldn't believe."

Taylor choked on a laugh and glanced over her should at Sammie. "Later. Maybe. Like, *much* later."

Sammie opened her mouth but whatever she'd been about to say was drowned out by the announcer's voice coming across the arena's speaker. Loud, deep and commanding. Booming with excitement, each word drawn out for maximum effect.

"Ladies and gentlemen, let's hear it for…your…Chesapeake Blades!"

chapter
TWENTY-ONE

Charles glanced over at Taylor, wondering why she was so quiet. She'd been this way for most of the night, ever since they'd left the arena. Before then, even, if he stopped to think about it. He had sensed something wasn't quite right when she was on the concourse, signing autographs with the rest of the team. Yes, she'd been smiling and laughing, posing for pictures and signing the stack of pucks and shirts Murphy had ordered for the event. But he'd seen the hint of shadows in her eyes, noticed the few times her smile had faded as she'd gotten a faraway look on her face.

Almost like the look she had gotten on her face when they were standing in the tunnel before hitting the ice. He'd known exactly what she was remembering. How could he not, when he was remembering the same thing? It was hard not to, not when everything was almost exactly the same as it had been twelve years ago. That's why he'd gone over to her, why he'd said what he did. Had he been too obvious? Let too much show? Maybe, because Murph had given him an odd look when he joined him again, after the team had moved out to the ice. But Murph hadn't said anything.

There wasn't anything he could say. There was no rule about fraternizing, nothing prohibiting it. Maybe there should be. Maybe there *would* be. But right now, there wasn't.

And it wasn't like they weren't being discreet. They were.

But none of that had anything to do with Taylor's uncharacteristic silence.

He lowered himself to the leather sofa and held out the glass of wine he had just brought in from the kitchen. Taylor took it, her lips curling in a brief smile of thanks, then simply sat there, holding it, that faraway look in her eyes again.

He shifted closer and draped one arm around her shoulders then pulled her closer.

"I think tonight went fairly well, don't you?"

Taylor nodded and took a sip of wine, then cradled the glass between both hands. "Yeah. It was good."

"There was a nice turnout for the autographs. Another good sign."

"Yeah. Good."

Charles swallowed a sigh and ran his fingers through the length of her hair, watching as the soft light played on the silky strands. Taylor didn't move, just sat there staring into her glass of wine.

He sat back and nudged her knee with his own, waiting until she finally looked over at him. "What's wrong?"

"Nothing. Why?"

"Because you didn't brush my hand away when I started playing with your hair. Because you're just sitting there, looking like you're lost and lonely." He ran the tip of his finger along the bare skin of her forearm, across her wrist to her fingers. She released her hold on the wine glass and curled her fingers around his own, her grip loose.

"Come on, out with it. What's wrong?"

Her brows lowered over her shadowed eyes as she shook her head. "Nothing's wrong."

"You know I'm not buying that, right?"

A few minutes went by, filled with nothing but the soft strains of music coming from the sound system across the room. He waited, watching as Taylor shifted on the sofa, that odd frown on her face—like she was trying to figure something out, only she wasn't quite sure what it was. She started to raise the glass to her lips, hesitated, then leaned forward and placed it on the glass coffee table in front of them. Her shoulders heaved with the force of her deep breath as she turned and faced him.

"How can you even stand to be with me?"

The question surprised him so much, he couldn't even blink. He tilted his head to the side, wondering if he had misunderstood, then leaned forward until their noses were almost touching. "I'm sorry. What? I don't think I heard—"

"You heard me." Taylor slid away from him, just enough to put a few inches of space between them. "How can you stand to be with me? After the way I treated you?"

Charles reached for his own glass of wine and

took a long swallow, trying to get his thoughts in order. It didn't help. "Am I missing something? After you treated me like what, *when?*"

Taylor folded her hands in her lap, her fingers twisting together. She stared at her hands for a long minute then released another heavy sigh and finally met his gaze. "When we were kids. I was such a cocky little shit, all those things I said to you—"

"Taylor—"

"And even a couple of months ago, when I first saw you again. And then—"

"Taylor—"

"I just don't understand how—"

Charles leaned forward and captured her mouth with his own, finally silencing her. She tensed under his kiss, but only for a second. Then she sighed into his mouth and leaned against him, her arms wrapping around his neck. And God, it would be so easy to lose himself in her kiss. Her touch. To lift her into his arms and carry her back to his room.

But not yet. They needed to talk. He needed to find out what was bothering her first, to find out what was behind her questions.

He gentled the kiss and eased away from her, then reached up and tucked a thick strand of hair behind her ear. "So what's going on? Why all the worries?"

"I just don't understand why you want to be with me after I was so mean."

"Are you talking about when we were kids?"

"Yeah. Mostly. But recently, too. When you first started working for the Blades."

"Why are you so worried about what happened twelve years ago?"

"Because I was so mean. And cocky." She leaned

back and stared down at her hands again. "I can't believe I was that awful—"

"Taylor, you weren't awful."

"How can you say that?"

"Because I was there, remember? We always got into it when were kids. But you never dished out more than you were handed. If you remember correctly, I wasn't exactly super nice to you, either."

"Yeah, but—"

"No *buts* about it. I was always teasing you, egging you on. But you never backed down. That's one of the things I liked about you."

"But—I was *mean*!"

Her face was screwed up into such a comical expression of dismay that Charles almost laughed. Not because it was funny—it wasn't. She was truly upset, convinced that she had been so awful to him all those years ago. But he remembered it differently, remembered how he'd been so jealous and intimidated. Remembered how he'd said his own share of mean things to her, teasing her, pushing her. Didn't she remember any of *that*?

He reached for her and pulled her closer, dropped his mouth on hers for a quick kiss. She narrowed her eyes, watching him with a mixture of confusion and uncertainty.

"You weren't mean."

"I was."

"Okay, then. You weren't the only one who was mean. Is that better?"

"No." She tried to pull away, gave up when he tightened his arm around her. "How can you even stand to be near me?"

"Are you honestly upset over something that

happened twelve years ago? When we were nothing but stupid kids who didn't know any better?"

"It doesn't say much for who I am."

He ran a hand through her hair then cupped her cheek. "Taylor, we were kids. It has nothing to do with who we are now."

"But—"

"Fine. If it still upsets you that much, I'll let you make it up to me."

She tilted her head back, the first hint of a smile teasing her mouth. "Why do I get the feeling that isn't as magnanimous a gesture as you want me to believe?"

"*Magnanimous*. Wow. Pretty big word for a jock."

"Hey—"

He pressed a kiss against her mouth, this one a little longer. "I'll still let you make it up to me if you want. Because I'm selfless and noble like that."

Taylor finally smiled—a full smile, one that brightened her face and danced in her eyes. She leaned closer, her mouth a breath away from his own. "I think I can manage that."

"Yeah?" Heat rushed through him, firing his blood as her hands drifted across his chest, her fingers undoing the buttons of his shirt. He watched as her eyes darkened, as her cheeks flushed and her mouth parted on a shallow breath. He reached up and closed his hand around her wrist, stopping her while his mind was still able to form coherent thoughts.

"You have a game tomorrow. Don't you need me to take you home so you can get ready?"

Taylor's eyes met his, their amber depths alight with desire. She shook her head and leaned forward, then ran the tip of her tongue against his lower lip. "No. I want to stay here."

"Are you sure?"

"Positive."

Charles may have growled, he couldn't be sure. And he didn't care, not when her mouth closed over his. Hot. Wet. Hungry. She reached between them, her fingers releasing the last few buttons of his shirt. She spread the material apart then ran her hands over his chest, each touch searing him. Branding him.

And God yes, he wanted nothing more than to be branded by this woman. Tonight. Tomorrow.

Forever.

He cupped her face between his palms and took control of the kiss, deepening it. Claiming her. She melted against him, giving herself to him even if she didn't realize it, not yet.

Charles pulled her across his lap then wrapped his arms around her and stood, carrying her back to his room. She slid down his body, her heated gaze almost shy as she stepped away and peeled her clothes from her body. They landed in a careless pile at the foot of the bed, quickly covered by his own. Then she was in his arms again and they were falling against the mattress, their bodies entwined, their hands searching with frantic need. Soft curves, toned muscle. Valleys and peaks. Charles couldn't stop touching her, would never be able to feed the hunger blazing through his veins.

He pulled away long enough to stretch across the bed and reach into the nightstand drawer. His fingers closed around a foil packet and he ripped it open, held his breath when Taylor took it from him. She rolled the condom down the hard length of his erection, her fingers trembling against the sensitive flesh. Then she fell to her back, pulling him on top of her, the same need he felt flashing in the depths of her warm eyes.

His mouth crashed against hers. Hungry, desperate. He couldn't get enough of her, not even when he plunged into her tight heat.

Losing himself.

Finding himself.

chapter
TWENTY-TWO

Crowds usually never bothered him. People yelling and pushing. The press of bodies as everyone moved about, trying to do their own thing. It was nothing more than a part of everyday life.

But this...this was something completely different. Something totally out of his comfort level.

Charles shifted on the overstuffed sofa and looked around the spacious room, trying to take everything in. It was sensory overload: the running, the carrying-on, the shouts and laughter. He blinked, trying to bring everything into focus, but it was too much. He didn't know *where* to focus, didn't know which conversation to concentrate on. Hell, at this point, he wasn't even sure if he could *think*.

When Taylor had invited him to Sunday dinner with her family, he had imagined a quiet gathering. Casual conversation around the dinner table, maybe. Or maybe sitting around the living room talking with the television on in the background, the sound muted or turned down so low it didn't interfere with conversation. He'd even expected a third-degree interrogation of sorts. But he had never expected this…this *chaos*.

Five kids, ranging in age from four to eleven, ran around the spacious room, making it feel smaller somehow. Four girls and one boy. Two sets of twins. He glanced over, frowning as he tried to remember their names. The older girls were Taylor's sisters. The younger girls and small boy were her cousins. That was all he managed to remember. And he couldn't tell the twins apart, no matter how many quirky memory tricks he tried. Did it matter? Probably not. But at least it gave him something to focus on besides the two men sitting adjacent to him, studying him with stony faces.

Sonny LeBlanc and JP Larocque. Taylor's father and her uncle. He'd met both men before, of course, almost two months ago when they had come to the rink for that one disastrous news piece. And he remembered them from when he was a kid, playing youth hockey with Taylor. But this was different. He wasn't here to do any marketing or to discuss the Blades; he wasn't here to reminisce about old times.

He was here as Taylor's date.

Heat filled his face as the word swirled through his mind. Taylor's *date*. Her *date*. Or maybe he was more than just her date. You didn't bring casual dates to your parents' home for dinner. You didn't introduce casual dates to your family.

There was something almost comforting about that thought, once he got past the panic the idea created. Or maybe the panic was nothing more than survival instinct kicking in under the scrutiny of the two men next to him.

Charles tightened his hand around the bottle he'd been gripping for the last fifteen minutes. He wanted nothing more than to lift the bottle to his mouth and take a long swig of the beer, hoping it would steady his nerves—but he didn't dare. He didn't think it would make a good first impression if he upended the bottle and chugged it down. And it wouldn't look good if he ended up spilling it all down the front of his shirt, either. So he just sat there, his hand wrapped around the bottle so tightly that his fingers were starting to cramp.

This would be so much easier if Taylor was actually here but she wasn't. She had disappeared into the other room not long after they got here, right after making quick introductions and leaving him to the mercy of the wolves.

Abandoning him.

Maybe that was a slight exaggeration. Charles had no doubt that she was in the other room, talking with her mother and aunt—probably about him. Or maybe she was being interrogated, too. But at least her interrogation was being done without the background noise of screams and laughter coming from five kids.

Sonny LeBlanc shifted in the chair and leaned forward, pinning him with a steady gaze from steel gray eyes. "I noticed someone filming the game earlier. Who was it?"

"We, uh—" Charles stopped to take a deep breath and clear his throat. He couldn't stutter or riddle his answer with awkward pauses and hesitant *uh's* and *um's*.

Pretend this is nothing more than a press conference.

He cleared his throat again and started over. "We've started live streaming the games on social media, hoping to tap into the market that way. To build up some excitement. None of the networks have shown any interest in airing the games so we decided to take matters into our own hands."

"Has there been any success?"

Depends on how you define success.

But Charles didn't say that out loud. "Some. Today was the first game so I'm still waiting for the final numbers to come in."

Sonny leaned back in the chair, his gaze still focused on Charles. "Damn shame the Blades lost."

"Dad! This isn't a locker room!" One of the older girls—he wasn't sure which one—ran over to Sonny and held her hand out, palm up. Amusement flashed through Charles and he had to bite back a smile when the bigger man grumbled and reached into his front pocket. He pulled out some crumpled bills and placed one into the upturned palm. Charles looked closer, something like amazement shooting through him. Was the bigger man actually blushing? Yes, he was. Charles looked away, but not before the other man noticed him watching.

"I, uh, I have to pay them if they catch me swearing."

"Not that it helps any, eh?" JP laughed and clapped the older man on the shoulder. He turned toward Charles, humor flashing in his eyes. "This live streaming. It will help, you think?"

"That's certainly the hope, yes. Like I said, today was the first time. We'll continue doing it, even for the road games. The reach should continue to grow, especially when we combine it with a focused marketing for each demographic we're targeting."

Two blank faces stared back at him.

"I'm expanding our marketing reach now that I've got a budget to work with. Different age groups. Different neighborhoods. Men. Women. The young adult market. Things like that."

"Good. It would be a da—" Sonny stopped and glanced over at five expectant faces then cleared his throat. "It would be a shame if the Blades only played for one season."

"I don't intend to let that happen. The exhibition and autograph session yesterday was extremely well-received. My hope is that it opened the doors to an existing market that's more than ready for women's hockey. I'm working with the Banners' marketing department for more opportunities like that."

"That's good to know. If there's anything we can do to help, just let us know."

Charles nodded his thanks, some of his earlier discomfort fading—until Sonny leaned forward again, those gray eyes impaling him.

"How long have you been seeing my daughter?"

"Uh…um—" And just like that, Charles was transported back to the time when he was an awkward teenager. He shifted on the sofa, his gaze darting around the suddenly quiet room. It felt like seven sets of eyes were on him. Watching. Studying. Scrutinizing.

Probably because they were.

He shifted again and finally met Sonny's direct gaze. "Almost two months. Sir."

"Because she hasn't mentioned you at all. Didn't say anything about you until she called this morning to tell us she was bringing you to dinner after the game."

The words stung more than they should, for reasons that didn't make sense. Logically, he knew there had been no reason for Taylor to talk to her family about him. This thing they were doing—relationship, not *thing*—was still new. It hadn't even started in the way normal relationships did, with one or two dates, then a few more, then a few more after that. They had started with some friction, a little head-butting. And then things just sort of happened from there.

No, it didn't surprise him that Taylor hadn't mentioned him. Hell, he hadn't mentioned her to his family, either. The difference was, his family consisted solely of his mother, and he didn't talk to her as often as he should. Taylor's family, on the other hand, was much bigger and definitely a lot closer.

Yes, the words stung. But he thought that maybe that was the point. Thought that maybe Sonny was testing him somehow. Or pushing. Or trying to get a reaction.

He met Sonny's piercing gaze, ready to reply, hoping whatever words came out of his mouth would make sense and not make him sound like a blithering idiot. He was saved from answering when Taylor entered the room, amusement curling the corners of her mouth.

"I didn't say anything, Dad, because I knew you'd act like this. And I *did* kind of mention him. You remember." Taylor paused, her gaze catching his. Charles saw the laughter dancing in her eyes and knew what was coming. He wanted to jump up and stop her but it was too late—not that he'd be able to stop her anyway.

"No, Pumpkin, I don't remember."

"Sure you do." Her grin widened. "When I was doing all that complaining about Chuckie-the-fart."

chapter
TWENTY-THREE

"So am I the only one who thinks this is weird?"

"No, it's definitely fucking weird."

"Yeah, totally weird."

Taylor grabbed her gear bag from the luggage compartment of the bus then stepped back to join Sammie, Shannon, and Dani. All four of them stood on the cracked asphalt beside the bus, their gazes resting on the group of suits standing near the front.

The majority owner of the Blades, James Murphy. Two of the minor owners, or stakeholders, or whatever they were called, Mike Henderson and Owen Smith.

And Chuckie.

The four men had shown up with the rest of the team before the crack of dawn this morning, just before they were getting ready to head out for their road game in New York. It had come as a complete surprise to everyone—including Taylor. Chuckie hadn't said anything to her about going with them today. Judging from his appearance—tired, just a little worn around the edges—she wondered if maybe he had been called at the last minute. She had no way of knowing, and she hadn't been about to go up and ask him, not when he was sitting at the front of the bus with Mr. Murphy and the other two men.

"So why do you think they're here?"

"No idea." Shannon pushed the sunglasses to the top of her head, anchoring them in her thick blonde hair, and looked over at Taylor. "Your hottie didn't say anything to you?"

"He's not my *hottie*. And no, he didn't."

"Hunh. Wonder why not. You should go ask him."

"I'm not going to go ask him." Taylor looked over at the men once more, her gaze locking with Chuckie's. He offered her a quick smile, one that looked tired and strained, then turned away when Mr. Murphy said something to him.

"You're not curious?"

"Of course, I'm curious. That doesn't mean I'm just going to stroll right up and ask him. They're busy. See?"

"They don't look busy to me. They look like they're just standing around, shooting the shit."

"You mean like we're doing?" Sammie readjusted the grip on her bag then started walking backward toward the arena. "Come on, let's get inside. I need to pee."

"Why didn't you use the bathroom on the bus?"

"Ewww. Gross. No way. Besides, I didn't need to go then."

They followed Sammie, falling in with the rest of the team as they made their way across the parking lot.

Taylor noticed that everyone—including the coaches—kept throwing speculative glances at the four men.

Shannon caught up to Sammie, mimicking each step the shorter woman took: a hop, a skip, a little bounce. "The bathroom wasn't gross. I mean, it's practically new. You should have tried it out. You know, instead of dancing around like that."

"I'm not dancing." Sammie bounced from one foot to the other. "I just need to really pee."

"You want some water?"

"No!"

"You sure?" Shannon pulled a nearly-full bottle from her bag and shook it in front of Sammie. "Because there's nothing like a nice cold bottle of really wet water trickling down your throat and hitting your full bladder when you need to pee."

"Oh God, stop." Sammie turned and started to run, rushing to the double doors and nearly knocking Coach Reynolds off her feet.

Taylor bit back a laugh and elbowed Shannon in the side. "Why do you do that to her?"

"Seriously? Because she's fun to tease. Duh." Shannon looked over her shoulder, a speculative frown creasing her face. "So why do you think they're really here?"

"I don't know. Maybe Mr. Murphy really wants to take an interest now. I mean, we got the ice fixed. And we don't have to drive around in that death-trap anymore, worrying about suffocating to death on exhaust fumes."

"Yeah. That's something, I guess. Still don't understand why they decided to come with us, though."

Dani pushed between them. "Maybe he wants to act like a real owner. You know, like the pros. I heard lots of the owners travel with their teams."

"I guess."

Taylor grabbed the door and held it open for the other two. "Stop worrying about it. Them being here doesn't mean anything. I mean, we still need to just focus on the game."

"But that's the problem. I couldn't do my thing on the bus with them there. They're fucking up my mojo."

"Your mojo is fine." Dani pushed Shannon through the door with a laugh. "And nobody was stopping you from doing anything so stop being so freaking weird."

"Hey. I'm not weird. I just have a routine. And I get antsy when anyone messes with it."

"Nobody was messing with anything."

They filed into the locker room with everyone else, the noise level automatically increasing as their voices bounced off the cracked and faded concrete walls and floors. The odor of musty water and stale, sweaty gear made Taylor wrinkle her nose, but only for a minute. This was a smell she was accustomed to, one she had been smelling for more than half her life. It was usually just the first whiff that caught her off-guard.

Usually. This odor was a bit stronger than normal, though.

"Oh God." Dani pinched her nose, her face scrunched up in distaste. "When's the last time they aired this room out?"

"Probably never." Taylor tossed her bag on the bench and started pulling gear out, arranging everything into a neat pile. Sammie appeared next to her and dropped to the bench, a frown marring her face.

"I should have used the bathroom on the bus."

"That bad, huh?"

"Yeah. Worse, even. I'm seriously thinking of skipping a shower after the game."

"It's really that bad?"

"Oh yeah. Makes me appreciate what we have back home, you know?"

Taylor nodded in silent agreement. Just over a month ago, she would have disagreed. She would have argued and said that what they had was next-to-nothing, that it didn't come close to what the pro teams—or even the semi-pro teams—had. But that was a month ago and things had changed. Her own attitude had changed. She wasn't afraid to hope anymore, wasn't afraid to think that maybe this whole new league might actually lead to something.

That it might actually *become* something.

They still had a long way to go and there were still a million and one obstacles to overcome, but it was a start. And it was definitely better than nothing. So maybe, just maybe, things would work.

Maybe.

She pushed the thoughts from her mind and focused on getting dressed, slipping into her pre-game zone so she'd be ready to hit the ice when the game started. The rest of the team was doing the same, following whatever small rituals they had established over time.

Dani, sitting in a corner, her legs crossed as she listened to music while she meditated.

Sammie, staring at the picture of Clare tucked inside her helmet, her lips moving soundlessly.

Jordyn, wrapping her stick with bright tape in an intricate pattern that meant something only to her.

Even Rachel and Amanda, coming out of the bathroom with their arms around each other's shoulders, their heads close together in quiet conversation. Taylor frowned. Maybe that wasn't so much a ritual as them just being themselves. She looked closer, frowning, wondering why it looked like Rachel was propping Amanda up.

Taylor didn't have time to dwell on it, not when it was time to line up and head out to the ice. Probably just her imagination, anyway.

Her mind turned elsewhere, focusing on stretching her muscles as they warmed up. Then the ice was cleaned and it was time to line up for the anthem and start the game. She glanced around at the nearly nonexistent crowd, told herself not to worry about it, then took her spot at center ice, falling into position beside Dani for the puck drop. Knees bent, back limber, stick held at the ready in three, two, one—

Dani won the face off and shot the puck behind her, toward Jordyn. She took off down the ice, her stride long and easy, then passed the puck to Taylor. Back and forth, gaining speed, only to lose the puck and have to chase it down the ice again.

The first period flew by, only minutes left with no score on the board. Taylor was back on the ice again, along with Dani and Rachel.

Sweat coated Taylor's face, her legs burning as she raced toward their own net. One of the players from New York took a wild shot. Shannon deflected the puck with her stick, sending it flying to the side.

Taylor raced for it, crashing into the boards and nearly falling. She righted herself and spun around, digging into the corner for the puck, her jaw clenched in determination. She got a piece of it, broke free from the tangle of players, and looked behind her a split-second before shooting it toward Amanda.

The puck slapped against the blade of Amanda's stick and bounced up, hitting her in the chest. Amanda brushed it away, knocking it back to the ice, then cradled it with her stick and headed away from their net. Taylor and Rachel followed, getting ahead of her, fighting to get open so Amanda could pass it to one of them.

Amanda looked up, her eyes narrowed behind the cage of her helmet, then pulled back on her stick. But instead of passing the puck, she kept falling backward, an odd vacant expression on her face. Taylor watched as she hit the ice and lay there, not moving.

Play continued, the other team racing in for the loose puck. Taylor dropped her stick and called to the ref, signaling for a stop in play as she hurried over to Amanda's prone body. Rachel and Dani slid to their knees behind Taylor, the echo of their breathing harsh in the sudden silence surrounding them.

"Amanda. Amanda, can you hear me?" Taylor leaned closer, her hands shaking as she ripped off her gloves and reached for Amanda. She didn't touch her, she was afraid to, had no idea what was wrong with her. She was just lying there, her eyes partially rolled back behind half-opened lids. Her face was pale, her lips tinged an odd gray, her chest barely moving.

Shouts echoed around them as more people joined them on the ice. Coach Reynolds. Two of the refs. The coach from the New York team. Two paramedics, dressed in blue jumpsuits, shuffled out to the ice, heavy equipment bags in their hands.

Someone reached for Taylor, pulling her out of the way, helping her to her feet as the paramedics knelt beside Amanda.

"What is it? What's wrong?"

Coach Reynolds eased them away, her face a grim mask. "Blades, all of you. Back to the bench. Take a knee."

"What's wrong with Amanda? What happened?"

"You!" Rachel grabbed Taylor's arm, her grip hard and bruising. "This is your fault."

"What? I didn't—"

"Ladies, I said back to the bench. Now."

"It's your fault, LeBlanc." Rachel kept talking, her face twisted in anger and agony. "You hit her with the puck. This is your fault."

"No. It wasn't—" Taylor stopped, fear gripping her, chilling her. She looked back at Amanda, her body still and unresponsive as the paramedics worked on her.

Was this her fault? Had Amanda been hurt because of her? No, it couldn't be. Taylor hadn't hit her with the puck. The shot wasn't that hard. It had just bounced up. A fluke. Something that happened all the time.

But if it wasn't her fault, then what had happened? Why was Amanda just lying there, not moving? It *had* been her fault. There was no other reason. None.

Taylor pulled her arm from Rachel's grip and dropped to her knees, her legs no longer able to support her weight as one of the paramedics started chest compressions on Amanda's limp body.

chapter
TWENTY-FOUR

The crack at her feet seemed to grow, the small line expanding, stretching, getting bigger and bigger as she watched. A drop of water fell onto it, spreading out until it disappeared into the blackness.

Taylor kept focusing on that crack, urging it to open up, to swallow her whole and take her away from the noise and lights that threatened to send her over the edge.

Another drop fell onto the crack, then another, disappearing the way the first one had. Her vision swam and blurred as the chill slammed into her. Her legs started shaking, then her arms and hands, the chill growing colder, claiming her until her entire body shook. Until her teeth started chattering, the sound of enamel grating against enamel loud in her ears.

She felt something touch her, a small warmth on her shoulder that made no sense at first. Words, quiet and strained, were lost in the surrounding noise. Her chest tightened, invisible steel bands squeezing until she had to fight to breathe.

She didn't want to fight. She just wanted to fall into the crack. To disappear into the blackness. To pretend none of this was happening, that it was nothing more than a bad dream.

But it wasn't. Taylor knew, somewhere deep in the back of her mind where reason fought to surface, that she wouldn't be able to wake from this. There would be no second of startled breath, no moment when she launched herself out of bed only to realize the nightmare was behind her. That the horror was nothing more than her imagination.

This was real. Too real.

Someone grabbed her hand and folded her fingers around something warm. Unwelcome heat seeped into the flesh of her palm, pulling her attention away from that dark crack at her feet.

"Taylor. You need to drink this. Please."

The words reached her through a foggy haze of numbness, pulling more of her attention away from the crack that beckoned and called. Taylor blinked, her vision clearing, then slowly straightened in the hard, plastic chair. She noticed the cardboard cup of black coffee in her hand, noticed a smaller hand cradling hers, helping her hold the cup so she wouldn't drop it.

Sammie. Sammie was sitting next to her, brown eyes wide with worry, the fragile skin beneath them dark with smudges. Taylor nodded, thinking that was what Sammie wanted her to do, then raised the cup to her mouth and took a small sip.

Liquid scalded her tongue, her throat. It should hurt, she knew that on some level, but she didn't feel it. She couldn't feel anything but the cold that held her in its grip.

"It's not your fault, Taylor. Do you hear me? It's not your fault." Sammie repeated the words, her voice rough and urgent, like she was intent on making Taylor believe.

Taylor shook her head, knowing Sammie was lying. It *was* her fault. All of it.

They were gathered in the waiting room at the hospital, had been there for what seemed like hours. All of them: the entire team, the coaching staff. Even the owners and Chuckie. They were huddled together, talking quietly.

Everyone except Taylor. She was seated across the room, in a corner by herself, needing to be alone. Knowing this was her fault. They wouldn't be here—Amanda wouldn't be here—if it hadn't been for her.

It was her fault and she needed to be alone, needed to think about what happened, needed to figure out what she'd done while they waited to hear about Amanda.

But Sammie wouldn't leave her alone. She kept talking to Taylor, rambling words that made no sense. Couldn't Sammie tell she needed to be alone? She needed to tell her that. Needed to tell her she should go over with the rest of the team, to sit with them as everyone stared at her, whispered about her. Talked about how she'd hurt Amanda.

But she couldn't get the words out, couldn't even form them in her head. Everything was too thick, too hazy and foggy.

"It's not your fault, Taylor."

Taylor nodded, trying to tell Sammie once more that it was, but she still wouldn't listen. She tightened her hand around Taylor's and guided the cup back to her mouth, forcing her to take another sip.

"No, I don't want—"

"Taylor, please. Just drink it."

"I said no." Taylor pushed the cup away, ignoring the dark liquid that sloshed over the rim and landed on her jersey. She heard Sammie's ragged sigh, felt loneliness wrap itself around her when Sammie finally got up and left.

Taylor wrapped her arms around her middle and leaned forward, her gaze seeking the crack under her feet, wishing once more that she could just disappear into its depths. A shadow darkened the floor in front of her but Taylor didn't look up. She didn't want to look up, she wanted to be left alone.

The shadow moved to the side, out of her line of vision. The chair next to her creaked and groaned as someone sat down. Then an arm draped around her shoulders and tugged, pulling her toward a solid wall of comforting heat.

Taylor squeezed her eyes shut and shook her head. She wanted to scream, to say she wanted to be left alone, but she couldn't force the words through her clogged throat.

Strong arms closed around her, holding her tight. Hands, large and gentle, rubbed soothing circles against her back. A voice, deep and warm, whispered words of comfort in her ear. Chuckie's voice. Chuckie's arms, solid and reassuring. Taylor fisted one hand in his shirt and buried her face in his shoulder, tears burning her eyes and throat. How long did she sit there, crying, unaware of the noise and stares and whispers?

She didn't know. Wasn't even aware of them until the air shifted around her. Until the noise drifted off, fading into an oppressive silence laced with anxious expectancy.

Taylor lifted her head, her bleary gaze drifting around the room until it came to a stop at the small group gathered by the metal door leading back to the emergency room. An older man dressed in scrubs, his face lined with weariness, stood next to Mr. Murphy and Coach Reynolds, talking quietly. Relief flashed across Coach Reynolds' face, the emotion quickly replaced by concern and something that looked like anger.

The coach's gaze darted to Taylor then snapped away, landing on Rachel Woodhouse. The coach nodded, said something to Mr. Murphy, then headed toward Taylor, her steps strong and filled with purpose.

Taylor's breath hitched in her chest, her lungs burning. Chuckie's arms tightened around her as the coach stopped in front of them, brows pulled low over her pinched eyes.

"Beall's going to be fine."

Relief surged through Taylor, releasing the steel bands that had been constricting her lungs. She sucked in a deep breath, her head swimming. "Really? She's okay?"

"She will be. And this had nothing to do with you, LeBlanc. Absolutely nothing."

"But the puck—"

"It wasn't that. Not even close."

"Then...I don't understand. What happened? What was it?"

Coach's mouth pursed into a thin line, like she didn't want to say. Her gaze drifted to Chuckie, settling on him for a long minute. Then she sighed and looked back at Taylor, resignation and regret reflected in her eyes. "An overdose."

She turned on her heel and stormed across the room, heading straight for Rachel. The other woman's face drained of all color as she backed away, her gaze scanning the room as if she was looking for a way to escape. Her eyes landed on Taylor, the expression of fear and hatred startling her. Coach Reynolds stepped in front of Rachel, said something in a low voice, then led her out of the room.

Taylor sagged against Chuckie, her body limp and drained as confusion swirled through her mind. "Overdose? Did she really say that?"

"Yeah."

Taylor turned toward him. "But how? Why?"

Chuckie shook his head then leaned forward and pressed a quick kiss against her forehead. His arms tightened around her for a brief second then he released her and stood up. He motioned toward Sammie, who hurried over to them.

"I have no idea but I need to talk to Murph, find out what's going on."

Sammie lowered herself into the empty chair with a heavy sigh. "She's going to be okay?"

"Yeah. Sounds like it."

"What happened? Did Coach say?"

Taylor hesitated, not sure if she should say anything. She decided against it, even if everyone would find out the truth eventually. "Not really, no. Just that it wasn't my fault."

Sammie flashed a quick smile at her, one filled with weary relief. "Well I already knew that. So now what?"

"I don't know." And she didn't. What did they do now? Just go on like nothing happened?

Taylor pulled in another shaky breath and focused

on the two men standing off to the side, their heads bent together in deep conversation. She didn't have to look close to see the tension in Chuckie's shoulders, or the angry determination on Mr. Murphy's face.

And she couldn't shake the feeling that something was about to change—for all of them.

chapter
TWENTY-FIVE

Something was going on. Taylor didn't know what, but the sickening knot in her stomach told her it wasn't good. It was obvious that her teammates felt it, too. Everyone was off tonight, worse even than they'd been Tuesday night.

Taylor skated over to the bench and leaned over to grab a bottle of water. Not because she was thirsty—she hadn't been working hard enough to break more than the smallest of sweats—but because it gave her a chance to look around the ice and watch everyone without being obvious.

It also gave her a chance to get closer to where the big meeting was happening off to the side. Mr. Murphy was there, along with a few of the other co-owners, and the entire coaching staff. Taylor couldn't tell what they were talking about, they were too far away. But she could read their body language, see the anger on Mr.

Murphy's face and the abrupt motions Coach Reynolds kept making with her hands.

Definitely not good.

She raised the bottle to her mouth and took a long swallow then shifted her body at an angle that gave her a view of both the ice and the meeting. The other players were watching as well, only making the smallest pretense of practicing.

And they needed the practice, not just so they could start coming together again as a team. They needed it to take their minds off what had happened at Saturday's game in New York and the news they had learned at Tuesday night's practice.

Amanda Beall had overdosed on a cocktail of recreational drugs she had been taking for a while. Mr. Murphy and the coaching staff may have wanted to keep that a secret, but it had been blasted all over the media by Sunday. And on Tuesday, the team learned that Amanda was no longer part of the Blades. She'd been kicked off the team, her contract terminated, no questions asked. Taylor wasn't sure how she felt about that—about any of it.

Shouldn't they have at least offered to help her? Had that even been an option? She didn't know. She didn't think anyone knew, except maybe Rachel.

And Rachel wasn't talking.

Taylor glanced over at the other woman, watching her go through the motions of a shooting drill. Her movements were sluggish, unenthusiastic; her shots were weak and wide. Which meant absolutely nothing because the rest of the team was the same way, doing nothing more than just going through the motions.

As Captain, it was her job to run practice tonight—at the request of Coach Reynolds. It was also her job to get the team excited, to build up their enthusiasm. To tighten the bonds that had been damaged from the events on Saturday.

That's what she *should* be doing, but her heart wasn't in it any more than the rest of the team. Not with this heavy pall of negativity hanging over them.

Taylor tossed one final glance at the tense meeting happening on the other side of the glass then flung the bottle behind the bench. She had an idea, but she wasn't sure if it would work or not. At the very least, it might take everyone's mind off the group of suits huddled together with the coaches.

She pushed off the boards and skated toward center ice, waving Sammie and Dani and a few of the other girls in. They slid to a stop in front of her, their gazes filled with curiosity.

Dani looked over at the small group then frowned at Taylor. "Any idea what they're talking about?"

"No. I wasn't close enough to hear. But none of them look happy—especially Coach."

"You think this is about Amanda?"

"I don't know. I don't think so. I mean, they already kicked her off the team. Why would they still be talking about her?"

"If they're not talking about her, then what the hell are they discussing?"

"Whatever it is, it looks serious." Sammie took a deep breath then let it out in a rush, her shoulders deflating with the move. "I don't like it. I've got a really bad feeling about it."

"Well, we'll find out eventually. I guess."

"Has Chuckie said anything?"

Taylor shook her head. There was no use denying that the two of them were together now, not when everyone had seen the way Chuckie was holding her at the hospital. She wasn't sure how she felt about that, how she felt about everyone knowing her personal business. It was too late to worry about it now, though, because there wasn't anything she could do about it.

"He's been busy doing damage control, trying to bury the negative press."

Dani snorted. "Yeah. Good luck with that."

Taylor ignored the comment, mostly because there was nothing to say, especially not when she agreed with it. "In the meantime, we need to do something to get everyone back on the same page. Do something to lighten everyone's mood."

"Like what?"

"How about some line dancing?"

Five faces looked at her with varying expressions of shock and disbelief. Sammie was the first one to speak, her voice pitched high in surprise.

"Line dancing? Seriously?"

"Sure, why not?"

"I thought we were supposed to be practicing."

"Look around, Sammie. Does it look like anyone is actually practicing? We need to do something to break through this thing and get us working together again. Get our minds off everything going on. Do you have any better ideas?"

"Well, no. But I'm not sure how we're supposed to line dance on skates."

"You'll figure it out." Taylor twirled the stick in her hand and looked around. "Anyone else have something better in mind?"

"Nope."

"Not me."

"Okay, line dancing it is then. I'll go find the radio.

Dani and Sammie, get everyone together. But don't tell them why, okay?"

"Why? Afraid of a mutiny?" Dani meant the words as a joke but they still hit home, knotting Taylor's stomach.

"You have no idea."

She headed back to the bench, wondering if she needed her head examined. Line dancing? Instead of practicing? Surely, she could have come up with something different. But her mind had completely blanked and it was the only thing she could think of besides running regular drills. And everyone had so much fun that night after their first game, when they'd gone to The Ale House, laughing and dancing and just cutting loose. *That* was what they needed right now, just something to have some fun and get their minds off everything else.

The shrill blare of a whistle stopped her in her tracks. She slid to a stop, spinning around as Coach Reynolds and Coach Chaney walked onto the ice, their faces lined with fury. Taylor's heart slammed into her chest, her stomach knotting with apprehension. Coach Reynolds glanced over at her then quickly looked away, blowing the whistle again.

"I need all of you over here. Now."

Everyone immediately raced to the boards, coming to a stop a few feet away from Coach Reynolds. Taylor saw the confusion on her teammates' faces and knew it mirrored her own. Did everyone else have the same knot of dread twisting their guts, or was that just her?

No, it was everyone. Like they all knew something was coming. Something bad.

Seconds stretched into minutes, drawing nerves

tight until Coach Reynolds released a heavy sigh and looked around, her gaze resting on each face for a split second before moving to the next one. She tossed an angry look over her shoulder then turned back once more.

"Everyone needs to line up and proceed to the restroom for a drug test."

Shocked silence greeted her words, then questions started flying, overlapping one another.

"What?"

"Whose idea was this?"

"They can't make us do that, can they?"

"Isn't that supposed to be done in a lab?"

Coach Reynolds held her hands up, signaling for silence. "This isn't my call and no, there's nothing I can do about it. As for a lab—" She stopped and looked over her shoulder again, her face red with anger.

"As for a lab, you'll be using home tests. These will be issued immediately and nobody is exempt."

"But Coach—"

"Not my call, ladies." She lowered her voice, regret flashing across her face. "I'm sorry. I wish there was something I could do."

"What fucking bullshit." Shannon ripped her helmet off and shot a withering glare in the direction of the men standing on the other side of the glass. "Are they going to watch, too?"

"Coach Chaney will be present, yes."

"Seriously? We have to pee in front of someone? I don't think I can!" Sammie's voice was filled with the same outrage and disbelief reflected on everyone's face.

Shannon let out a string of loud curses and stormed toward the door, throwing her helmet and stick down as she moved through it. She paused in front of the men and Taylor held her breath, wondering if Shannon was going to say or do something stupid. But she merely shook her head and swore again before heading to the bathroom.

Everyone else skated toward the doors, muttering words of disbelief and outrage. Taylor hesitated, wanting to say or do something, but knowing she couldn't. She started off the ice, only to have Coach Reynolds call her back.

"LeBlanc, I need a minute."

Taylor whirled around, the dread growing larger in her stomach. "Yes, Coach?"

"Not you."

"What do you mean? You said no exceptions."

"I did." Coach Reynolds moved closer, regret filling her eyes. "I'm sorry, Taylor, I tried. And if it was up to me—"

"What? What's going on?"

"You're suspended from the team. Indefinitely."

Taylor stood there, convinced she hadn't heard right. Suspended? No, she couldn't be. Her heart jumped to her throat, making it hard to breathe, hard to concentrate. She swallowed, trying to draw air into her burning lungs.

"I—I don't understand."

"Taylor—"

"Is this because of Amanda? I thought—this doesn't make sense. I don't understand."

"It's not because of Amanda. It's—" Coach looked away, her shoulders sagging. When she looked back, Taylor saw the sheen in her eyes, saw the angry set to her jaw. "It's because you're involved with someone in the front office."

"What?" The words came out as a strangled

choke. This was about Chuckie? Because they were seeing each other?

"Mr. Murphy thinks it would be best if you were no longer associated with the team, at least for the time being, given all the negative publicity that's happened as a result of the incidents that occurred on Saturday." Coach recited the long string of words, her voice dull and lifeless. She took a deep breath, anger flashing in her eyes. "I'm sorry, Taylor. It's bullshit. I tried to talk him out of it but...I'm sorry."

Anger sliced through Taylor, followed by the sharp pain of betrayal. She was being suspended, indefinitely, because she was seeing Chuckie. Had he known? No, he couldn't have. He would have said something.

Wouldn't he?

Taylor stood there for the longest time, her body numb, her heart threatening to explode in her chest. Everything she had worked for all her life, all her hopes and dreams, shattered. Destroyed.

Taken away from her.

Just like that. On a whim. With no thought.

How? Why? She didn't understand, couldn't make sense of it. She wanted to scream. To hit. To rail against the injustice. To fight back.

In the end, she simply skated off the ice, leaving the shattered pieces of her dreams behind her.

chapter
TWENTY-SIX

Charles flew up the steps, taking them two at a time until he skidded to a stop in front of Taylor's door. He banged his fist against it, making the metal shudder in the frame.

He paused, put his ear to the door and tried to listen for signs of movement inside. He couldn't hear anything over the pounding of his heart in his chest or the harsh rasp of each breath tearing from his lungs.

He pounded his fist against the door again. "Taylor. Open up. I know you're in there." She had to be. Her car was parked out front and he knew she wasn't working. She never worked Thursday nights because of practice.

Only she wouldn't be at practice ever again. Not anymore. Not after Murphy's stunt tonight.

How could he? Why the fuck would he do such a thing? What had he been thinking? Charles was still having trouble wrapping his head around it. Part of him wanted to believe it was some kind of sick joke, that Sammie had been playing a practical joke on him when she called earlier. But Sammie didn't joke, not like this. And there had been no mistaking the tears in her voice when she told him.

He had tried calling Murphy but the man wouldn't answer his phone. Then he tried calling Taylor but she refused to pick up, sending his calls straight to voicemail.

He banged on the door again, harder this time, desperation clear in his voice when he called out. "Taylor, please. Open the door."

Minutes went by before he finally heard the lock turn. The door opened, but only a few inches, stopped by the security chain. Taylor stared at him through one glazed eye rimmed in red. Hair hung in her face, covering most of the tear-streaked splotches along her cheek.

"Not now, Charles. Please." Her voice was thin and raspy, the words slightly slurred. But it was the use of his name, *Charles*, that sent his stomach plummeting.

She never called him *Charles*. Ever.

"Taylor, let me in. Please."

"I don't think—"

"Please."

She watched him through that single blurry eye for a long minute then closed the door. Charles held his breath, wondering if she'd unlock it and let him in—

Or if she had just sent him a message he wasn't willing to hear.

There was the faintest sound of metal sliding against metal, then the door opened again. He pushed through, not willing to give Taylor a chance to change her mind. The worry was misplaced because she was already heading for the loveseat, plopping down on it with a weary sigh. She reached for one of the throw pillows and pulled it to her chest, her head hanging low in dejection.

Charles stood just inside the door, his gaze taking everything in. Shadows filled the small apartment, the darkness broken only by the faint light coming from the bathroom at the end of the short hall. An open bottle of wine sat on the old trunk she used as a coffee table, a half-empty glass sitting next to it. A carton of melting ice cream, a spoon jutting out of the top, was shoved to the other side of the trunk.

Charles moved over to the loveseat and sat down next to her. It took all of his control not to pull her into his arms and hold her but her body language screamed *leave me alone*. He reached for her anyway then dropped his hand at the last second, letting it fall on the cushion between them.

"Sammie called me."

Taylor was quiet for so long, he wondered if she had heard him. Then she pulled in a quick breath and released it in a rush. "She shouldn't have."

"You're right. It should have been you who called me."

Taylor was quiet, too quiet. And she just sat there, not even bothering to look over at him. Charles clenched his jaw and bit back the disappointment flooding him.

"Why didn't you call me, Taylor?"

"I figured you already knew."

Her words sliced deep, sharper and more painful than any knife. He sat there, trying to breathe, refusing to believe her words. Refusing to think she actually believed them.

He shifted closer and reached for her hand, felt that invisible blade twist in his chest when she pulled away from him. "Taylor, look at me."

She still didn't move. He couldn't see her face, not with the way her hair was hanging down, shielding her. Charles waited, willing her to move. To look at him. To say or do something. Anything.

But she didn't.

He swore under his breath then moved off the loveseat and dropped to his knees in front of her. He reached out and cupped her face between his hands, his heart clenching at the cool dampness of her flesh. "Taylor, look at me."

She shook her head then averted her gaze when he tilted her head up.

"Taylor, please. You're killing me here. You have no idea what you're doing to me. Look at me. Please."

Long seconds stretched around them, filled with silence broken only by the pounding of his heart. Her body tensed and for one awful moment, he was afraid she'd pull away. That she'd reach out and push him or kick him or tell him to get out. To leave.

Then some of the tension seeped out of her and she raised her eyes, her gaze meeting his. His gut twisted at the pain and agony reflected in their depths. But that didn't hurt as much as the emptiness he glimpsed. Like she had given up. Like there was nothing left inside her.

He ran his tongue across his lower lip, trying to ignore the acid burning deep in his gut. "Tell me you don't believe that, Taylor. Tell me you don't really think I knew anything about this."

He held his breath, his eyes searching hers as he waited.

"I—" Taylor stopped and lowered her gaze, her teeth nibbling her bottom lip. A shudder went through her, her shoulders heaving with the force of her deep breath. She looked back up, moisture filling her eyes. "No, I don't."

Charles released the breath he'd been holding and pulled her into his arms, holding her tight. She felt frail, fragile, like all her inner strength—her dreams—had been ripped from her, leaving her empty and hollow, nothing more than a shell of the woman she'd been.

Long minutes went by before her arms wrapped around his waist. He could feel her body trembling, could hear each harsh breath as it was ripped from her lungs. And he could feel her tears against the skin of his neck as she cried, silent tears that wracked her body.

He stayed that way for a long time, simply holding her, whispering words of comfort and reassurance as she cried in his arms, until her body was limp from exhaustion.

Charles moved to his feet, adjusting his hold on her as he sat down and pulled her across his lap. She shifted, wrapped her arms around his neck, and dropped her head against his shoulder.

"I didn't know what he was planning, Taylor."

"I know." Her voice was quiet, ragged and hoarse, her breath nothing more than a whisper against his skin.

"I'll talk to him in the morning, find out—"

"No."

"Yes. This isn't right. He can't just—"

"It doesn't matter, Chuckie."

He leaned back, his gaze capturing hers. Did she see the anger and determination in his gaze? She must have. How could she not, when he was burning with it?

"The hell it doesn't. How can you even say that?"

"Because it doesn't."

"Bullshit. Hockey is your life, Taylor. You can't just give up."

"There's nowhere else to go."

"Yeah, there is. The Blades. I'll talk to him—"

"Chuckie, I don't want to play for them. Even if you do talk to him. After what he did? The way he treated everyone tonight, demanding that drug test? Then suspending me indefinitely? No. I'm done. It's over."

"The hell it is. Hockey is too important to you. I'm not going to just stand by and let you give it up."

Taylor reached up and ran her hand across his jaw, a look of such pure sadness in her eyes that he had to look away. "You don't have a say in the matter."

He took a deep breath, wondered if he was making the right decision, wondering what the chances were of his words backfiring on him. He turned back to her. He didn't try to hide his anger or disappointment. "So that's it? You're just going to give up? Quit?"

"I'm not quitting."

"That's what it looks like to me."

"I was suspended. That's not the same—"

"You just said you were. That you wouldn't go back to playing. What's that, if not quitting?"

Anger flashed in her eyes, but only for a second. "You're putting words in my mouth."

"No, I'm not. I'm just repeating what you said. You said you didn't want to play. That you were done. That it was over."

"That's not—"

"So you're quitting."

Anger flashed in her eyes again. She stiffened and pushed against him, trying to break his hold on her. Charles tightened his arms around her, refusing to let go.

"Chuckie, let me up."

"No. Not until you admit you're quitting."

"That's not what I said."

"Same thing."

"No. It's not." She pushed against him again then curled her hand into a fist and shoved it against his shoulder. "Let me up."

"Admit you're a quitter."

"No."

"Why? It's the truth."

"No, it's not. Let me go."

"Tell me."

"No."

"Admit it, Taylor."

She sagged against him, the fight leaving her body but still shining in her eyes. "Why are you doing this to me?"

"Because I want to hear you say it. I want you to prove me wrong."

Her gaze rested on his, her eyes filled with agony. Her voice was small, filled with uncertainty when she spoke. "Why?"

"Because the girl I had a on a crush on all those years ago would never quit." He eased one arm from behind her back and reached up, tucking the hair behind her ear. "And because the woman I fell in love with would fight for what she wanted."

Taylor stared at him for so long, he wondered if he had made a mistake. Yes, he had. He should have never said anything. It was too soon. She wasn't ready.

He shouldn't have thrown that at her, not tonight, not after everything else that had happened. Hell, maybe not ever. Maybe she didn't want to hear it. Maybe she didn't—

"You love me? But—why?"

"Why?" The word came out on a burst of choked laughter. "Because I'm a glutton for punishment."

"But—"

"Do me a favor: don't say anything, okay? Just pretend you didn't hear—"

Taylor's mouth crashed against his, her kiss hard and soft and almost desperate. He tightened his arms around her and took control of the kiss, deepening it, slowing her down when all he wanted to do was roll her body under his and claim her.

He finally pulled away, his ragged breathing matching hers. She watched him with wide eyes filled with wonder then leaned forward and rested her forehead against his.

"You love me." It was a statement, not a question.

"Yeah. I do."

"I—"

He reached up and pressed his fingers against her lips, silencing her. "I don't need to hear the words, Taylor. Not until you're ready. Not until you're sure. I know it's probably too soon for you. I don't expect—ouch." He pulled his fingers away from her mouth and looked down at them, surprised he didn't see bite marks in the flesh. "Shit. What the hell was that for?"

"For not letting me finish. And for assuming I don't know what I'm feeling or what I'm ready for." She pressed a quick kiss against his lips then leaned back, the corners of her mouth turned up in the sweetest smile he'd ever seen. "I love you, Chuckie. I thought I did but I wasn't sure until last week, right before we went out on the ice at the Banners' game."

Something tightened in his chest—not in pain, but in delight. He was helpless to stop the grin on his face, helpless to stop his hand from cupping her cheek. "Why then?"

"Because you remembered. And because of what you said."

"I meant it."

"I know you did." She leaned forward, her lips grazing his in a featherlight kiss. Then she sat back, her hand reaching for his, their fingers threading together. "But I don't know what to do about tonight. You're right, hockey's everything to me. What am I going to do if I can't play?"

"What did you do when we were kids and somebody said you couldn't do something?"

"Get angry and throw a fit?"

Charles laughed. "Yeah, okay. That too. But what else?"

"I don't—" Taylor hesitated, her head tilting to the side as she studied him. Amusement danced in her eyes, chasing away some of the shadows. "You mean, beat them up?"

"Yeah."

"You think I should go beat up Mr. Murphy?"

"Sure. Why not? And I'm going to tell you how to do it."

And he did, later that night as they lay curled in each other's arms.

chapter
TWENTY-SEVEN

Charles stood just outside the door and took a deep breath, trying to push the doubt to the side and completely out of his mind. Coming up with plans had never been a problem for him—and he'd been lucky, because most of the time, those plans worked. If they didn't, he learned from what went wrong, formulated a new one, and moved ahead until he found success.

Because he was good at what he did.

But if this one didn't work out—if it backfired or blew up in his face or any one of the other million things that could go wrong—there would be no second chance. No stepping back to reevaluate.

This was all or nothing.

It was the *nothing* part that terrified him.

He took another deep breath and let it out, nice and slow. He ran his hands along the front of his jeans, gave himself a mental shake and one final pep talk, then opened the door.

The office was quiet as usual—there wasn't enough staff for there to be any real noise. That also meant there weren't any witnesses. That could work in his favor.

If he was lucky.

He strode down the wide hall, past the tiny cubicle that passed for his office, and kept going. His was heading for the big office, the corner one with a view.

Murph's office.

The door was open—literally. Whether it was open figuratively remained to be seen. He knew the man meant well—in theory. Now it was time to put that theory to the test.

James Murphy was seated behind the small island that passed for his desk, dressed immaculately in a designer suit, looking every inch the part of a successful businessman. Mike Henderson and Owen Smith were sitting across from him, looking slightly bored as Murph's voice droned on about something. The tension was palpable, thick and heavy.

Was that a good sign? Or a bad omen?

Murph looked up, a frown creasing his weathered face when Charles stopped in the doorway. The steely eyes drifted over the jeans and sweatshirt Charles was wearing. Murph leaned back in the large leather chair, his thick white brows lifting in annoyance.

"Is it Casual Friday again?"

"I quit."

Murph's brows snapped together in a sharp frown and he leaned forward so fast, the leather chair bounced. It would have been funny—except there was nothing humorous about this whole thing.

"What the hell is all this about?"

"It's about you making my job impossible."

"I have no idea what you're talking about."

Charles shot a glance at the other two men then stepped forward and planted his fists on the edge of Murph's desk. "You brought me on to market this team yet you have thrown roadblocks my way at every turn."

"If this is about the budget, I already said I—"

"It's not about the budget, Murph. It's about that lamebrain stupid ass shit you pulled yesterday."

A stony expression crossed Murph's face. He sat back in the chair, exchanged a glance with the other two men, then slowly nodded. "I see. This is about your girlfriend."

"No, Murph. It's about you suspending the team's captain—who just happens to be one of your best players. It's about belittling the team by making them piss in a cup in front of witnesses. What the hell did you think that would accomplish?"

Owen Smith spoke up, his voice filled with condescension and disdain. "Those girls work for *us*. We pay them. After the debacle at last weekend's game, it was the right thing to do. As for your girlfriend—" A small smirk crossed his face. He propped his foot against his knee and smoothed the sharp crease of his pants leg. "We can't afford bad publicity. If the press found out that the players are screwing around—"

Charles reached down and grabbed the front of Owen's shirt, twisting his hand in the material and pulling him out of the chair. "You better be damn careful of what you say—"

"Enough!" Murphy's voice exploded around them, loud and booming. Charles clenched his jaw then released his hold on Smith, wondering if he had just totally fucked everything up.

Murph watched him, his steely gaze steady and calculating. *This* was the side of Murph that he'd heard about but hadn't yet seen—the shrewd businessman with a reputation for ruthlessness. And Charles couldn't get a read on the man, had no idea what he was thinking, not right now.

Murph leaned back in the chair and steepled his hands under his chin. He watched Charles for several long minutes, those gray eyes of his revealing nothing. "You do know that if you quit, nothing changes, right? There's nothing stopping me from hiring someone else to take your place."

"True." Charles waited several heartbeats then offered the other man a cool, calculating smile. "But you have to remember that marketing works both ways. And trust me, Murph, by the time you get someone else on board, there won't be much they can do to put a positive spin on this."

"Are you threatening—"

Murph sliced one hand through the air, silencing Owen. Several seconds went by, filled with tension, as Murph sized Charles up. Trying to figure out if he was bluffing? Possibly.

"I have to say I'm impressed, Chuck. I never expected this from you. Even if you follow-through with this...plan...what makes you think the team won't eventually recover?"

"Oh, I'm sure it could, given your money. The problem is that you won't have a team to market."

Direct hit.

Murph couldn't hide the surprise that flashed across his face. His gaze shot to the other two men then darted back to Charles. "What's that supposed to mean?"

"It means that you're one hell of a businessman, Murph, but you don't have a fucking clue when it comes to the bond that holds a team together." Charles straightened and moved to the window, tilting his head for Murph to join him. The older man reluctantly got to his feet and walked across the room, followed by Henderson and Smith.

The men gazed out the window, identical expressions of surprise etched on their faces. Down below, gathered in a show of solidarity, stood every single member of the Blades.

Taylor. Sammie. Shannon and Dani. Jordyn Knott and Rachel Woodhouse. Coach Reynolds and Coach Chaney. Everyone was there, all eighteen names on the roster.

"Son of a bitch." The strangled whisper came from Murphy and was laced with a hint of respect that surprised Charles.

"Most of them had to take off work to be here, Murph. That means losing a day's worth of pay—and none of them can afford that. That's how important this is."

"You're telling me they're ready to quit? Just like that?"

"Yeah, they are."

Owen Smith laughed, the sound cold and bitter. "Then let them. We can find other players—"

"Out." The single word was filled with cold authority. For one horrifying second, Charles was afraid Murph was talking to *him*, that the entire plan had backfired. But Murph was looking at the other two men, his stony expression leaving no room for argument.

Owen stepped closer, disbelief on his chalky face.

"Jim, we can find other players."

"No, you won't. Once word gets out, nobody will want to play for the Blades. Or you. It's happened before. Trust me, that's a PR nightmare you can't recover from—no matter how much money you throw at it."

"Jim—"

"Out. Both of you."

The other two men reluctantly left the office, closing the door behind them. Murph watched them leave then turned back and looked out the window. His face was carefully blank, unreadable.

"You definitely surprised me, Chuck. I didn't see this one coming." Murph turned away from the window and walked back to his desk. He leaned against it and crossed his arms in front of him, that thoughtful expression still on his face. "What are you going to do if I call your bluff?"

"What makes you think it's a bluff?"

"You're telling me the girls are ready to walk, just like that?"

"Yeah, they are. This is important to them."

Murph nodded then lowered his gaze, studying the top of his expensive Italian loafers for a long minute. He released a sigh then looked back at Charles. "What you said, about the bond—you're right. I don't know anything about it. When they first approached me about buying into this team, I thought it was a waste of money. Part of me still does. Lord knows we're not making anything back on the investment."

"It's still early—"

"Yes, it is. But I don't know many people who would blame me for cutting my losses now and getting out."

Dread twisted his gut. Charles hadn't considered that possibility and it took everything he had to stay upright, to not collapse in the chair next to him. If Murph noticed, he didn't show it.

"The problem, Chuck, is that I find being an owner of a sports team rather entertaining—even if it's not even considered a semi-pro team. I'd go so far as to say I find it a little rejuvenating for a man of my age." He pushed away from the desk and took a seat in the chair, his gaze thoughtful as he watched Charles. "It seems I have a bit of a dilemma."

"Only if you make it into one."

"I'm guessing you have a solution for me?"

Charles heaved a mental sigh of relief and made his way back to the desk. "Yeah, I do. Bring Taylor back. Apologize for pushing that stupid ass test on them last night—"

"For the record, that wasn't my idea. Owen meant well but I happen to agree with you."

"Then you shouldn't have listened to him."

"You're right, I shouldn't have. Anything else?"

"Yeah." Charles straightened, knowing this one could be pushing it. He didn't agree with it himself, but it would go a long way to repair the damage that had been done. "Put Amanda Beall back on the roster."

"I don't think—"

"Not active. Offer to help her with rehab. Make that a condition."

"I'm not sure—"

"It's a risk, I know. But it'll look good. And it will let the team know you're serious about making amends. It'll let them know you care."

"Hmm." Murph steepled his fingers under his chin again and looked away, his face creased in a thoughtful frown. Minutes stretched around them, filled with a heavy silence. Was there anything Charles could say to sway the decision? Or had he said enough already? He didn't know and for once, his instincts were oddly silent.

It didn't help that Murph's face was carefully blank and completely unreadable. He stood up, met Charles' gaze for a split second, then walked around the desk.

"Let's go talk to the girls."

chapter
TWENTY-EIGHT

"Are you sure this is going to work?"

"Yes." *Maybe.*

"What if it doesn't?"

"I don't know."

"We're fucked if it doesn't."

Everyone turned to look at Shannon but nobody said anything. There was nothing to say—she was right. If this didn't work, they were fucked.

Taylor curled her hands into tight fists and shoved them into the front pockets of her jeans. That might help stop them from trembling, but it did nothing to calm the nerves threatening to turn her stomach inside out. Would this work? There was so much at stake. It had to work.

She glanced around, studying the faces of her teammates surrounding her. Sammie. Shannon and Dani. Sydney and Maddison and Jordyn and Karly. Their coaches. Even Rachel, standing with them but just a little off the side.

These women weren't just her teammates—they had become her family. Dysfunctional, yes. Still getting to know one another, still working on their issues as they grew closer. But they were family nonetheless, held together with one common bond: their love of hockey.

And the desire to make something more of this tiny little chance they'd been given.

Willing to throw it all away if this desperate plan didn't work.

It *had* to work.

Jordyn nudged her then nodded toward the main doors of the small arena. "Here they come."

Stillness settled over the group as everyone turned toward the doors. Mr. Murphy walked out, looking every inch the shrewd businessman he had the reputation of being, with his tailored suit and neatly-trimmed white hair. What was going through his mind? She couldn't tell.

Chuckie walked out behind him, the total opposite in looks, wearing faded jeans and the old sweatshirt bearing the logo of his alma mater. His dark hair was mussed, his jaw covered with the shadow of day-old scruff.

And his face was as completely expressionless as Mr. Murphy's.

Taylor's stomach rolled, threatening to spill the light breakfast she'd forced down hours earlier. Sammie stepped closer, her trembling fingers gripping Taylor's arm with bruising strength.

"Oh, this doesn't look good. I think I'm going to be sick."

"At least you don't have to pee." Shannon

muttered the words under her breath, causing a ripple of nervous laughter. Sammie loosened her grip on Taylor's arm and shifted, turning to look at Shannon.

"I always have to pee."

More nervous laughter, the sound quickly fading as the two men approached them. Taylor's eyes darted to Chuckie but he wasn't looking at her.

And oh shit, that couldn't be good. If it was good, he'd let her know. Wouldn't he?

Mr. Murphy came to a stop in front of them, his gray eyes scanning each face. He turned toward Chuckie, some silent message passing between them, then faced the team once more.

"I understand you ladies are ready to walk out. To give this all up."

There was a long minute of silence before Shannon stepped forward, her chin thrust forward in challenge. "Yeah, we are."

"I see." Mr. Murphy clasped his hands behind his back and scanned their faces again, his gaze stopping on Taylor's. She saw the faintest glimmer of humor flash in the gray depths then he blinked and it was gone.

Maybe she had just imagined it.

"That would put me in quite a bind if you did."

Shannon stepped closer, her voice clear and strong. "That's not our problem."

A bark of laughter escaped the older man, surprising them all. "No. No, I guess it isn't."

Sammie's grip tightened on her arm again but Taylor barely noticed, not when she was so focused on Mr. Murphy, not when she was trying to control the hope threatening to break free.

The older man looked at her again, admiration

flaring in his eyes. Then he nodded, just once, before his lips twitched in a small smile.

"I admire anyone who's willing to stand up like you girls are doing. That takes guts." He glanced over at Chuckie, his lips twitching in that small smile again. "I've been told that I don't have a fucking clue about the bond that holds a team together. I trust that you girls are willing to teach me?"

Shannon moved one arm behind her back and shot everyone the thumbs-up sign. "Fuck yeah. If you're willing to learn."

Taylor choked back a groan. A few of the others gasped or muttered under their breath. Chuckie closed his eyes and reached up to pinch the bridge of his nose, his lips moving soundlessly.

Even Mr. Murphy seemed shocked into silence—but only for a few seconds. The smile that he'd been holding back broke free and he laughed then stepped toward Shannon. It looked like he was going to wrap his arm around her shoulder but he stopped at the last second, clapping her on the back instead. "I like you. You remind me of myself when I was younger."

"Is that a good thing?"

"Yes. Yes, it is." Mr. Murphy stepped back, sweeping them all with an amused glance. "Well, then. That's settled. Ms. Wiley and I will go discuss things that need to be changed and let the rest of you get back to work. I'll see everyone at tomorrow's game."

It took a few seconds for the words to sink in. Then there was a collective sigh of relief, followed by loud cheers and applause. The tension suddenly left Taylor, leaving her limp and light-headed and dazed. Sammie grabbed her in a huge hug, jumping up and down.

"Holy crappola! It worked. It worked! I can't believe it!" Sammie kept jumping up and down, shaking Taylor with each excited bounce. She stopped just as quickly as she started, a look of panic suddenly crossing her face. "Oh crap. I need to pee."

Sammie took off at a run, nearly knocking over Mr. Murphy and Shannon as she raced past them to get inside the arena. Taylor laughed, the sound fading on a rush of breath when Chuckie pulled her into his arms.

She melted against him, her body trembling in relief as his arms tightened around her. "You did it."

"Not me—*you*. All of you."

"But it was your idea." She leaned up and pressed a quick kiss against his mouth, then playfully whacked him on the arm. "You could have given me a sign, though. You had me worried because I couldn't tell what was going to happen."

"That was because I didn't know. Not for certain."

Taylor's eyes widened, a gust of chilled air swirling through her. "You seriously didn't know?"

"No, not at first. I had an idea but I wasn't sure."

"Oh God. I think I'm going to throw up—"

"No, you're not." Chuckie's arms tightened around her, supporting her. "You're stronger than that. You always have been."

"But it—"

He silenced her with a kiss. Long and gentle, one filled with promise. She was clinging to him, her head swimming and her heart overflowing with emotion when he pulled away—the same emotion flooding the deep ocean blue of his eyes when he looked at her.

Love. Clear and endless. Still new, but filled with promise and potential.

Chuckie reached up and tucked the hair behind

her ears, his mouth curling in that dangerously charming smile. "You did it, Taylor. It's a start. Baby steps, but I think this is the beginning of something that's going to be a lot bigger."

"You're right." She offered him her own smile and leaned against him. "It is."

They both knew she wasn't merely talking about the Blades.

###

Lisa B. Kamps

About the AUTHOR

Lisa B. Kamps is the author of the best-selling series *The Baltimore Banners*, featuring "…hard-hitting, heart-melting hockey players…" [USA Today], on and off the ice. Her *Firehouse Fourteen* series features hot and heroic firefighters who put more than their lives on the line and she's introduced a whole new team of hot hockey players who play hard and love even harder in her newest series, *The York Bombers*. *The Chesapeake Blades*--a romance series featuring women's hockey--launches in November 2017 with WINNING HARD.

Lisa currently lives in Maryland with her husband and two sons (who are mostly sorta-kinda out of the house), one very spoiled Border Collie, two cats with major attitude, several head of cattle, and entirely too many chickens to count. When she's not busy writing or chasing animals, she's cheering loudly for her favorite hockey team, the Washington Capitals--or going through withdrawal and waiting for October to roll back around!

Interested in reaching out to Lisa? She'd love to hear from you:

Website: www.LisaBKamps.com
Newsletter: http://www.lisabkamps.com/signup/
Email: LisaBKamps@gmail.com

Facebook:
https://www.facebook.com/authorLisaBKamps
Kamps Korner Facebook Group:
https://www.facebook.com/groups/1160217000707067/
BookBub:
https://www.bookbub.com/authors/lisa-b-kamps
Goodreads: https://www.goodreads.com/LBKamps
Instagram: https://www.instagram.com/lbkamps/
Twitter: https://twitter.com/LBKamps
Amazon Author Page:
http://www.amazon.com/author/lisabkamps

CROSSING THE LINE
The Baltimore Banners Book 1

Amber "AJ" Johnson is a freelance writer who has one chance of winning her dream-job as a full-time staffer: capture an interview with the very private goalie of Baltimore's hockey team, Alec Kolchak. But he's the one man who tries her patience, even as he brings to life a quiet passion she doesn't want to admit exists.

Alec has no desire to be interviewed--he never has, never will. But he finds himself a reluctant admirer of AJ's determination to get what she wants...and he certainly never counted on his attraction to her. In a fit of frustration, he accepts AJ's bet: if she can score just one goal on him in a practice shoot-out, he would not only agree to the interview, he would let her have full access to him for a month, 24/7.

It's a bet neither one of them wants to lose...and a bet neither one can afford to win. But when it comes time to take the shot, can either one of them cross the line?

Turn the page for an exciting peek at CROSSING THE LINE, available now.

"Oh my God, what have I done?" AJ muttered the phrase under her breath for the hundredth time. She wanted to rub her chest but she couldn't reach it under the thick pads now covering her. She wanted to go home and curl up in a dark corner and forget about the whole thing.

Me and my bright ideas.

"Are you going to be okay?"

AJ snapped her head up and looked at Ian. The poor guy had been given the job of helping her get dressed in the pads, and she almost felt sorry for him. Almost. Between her nervousness and the threat of an impending migraine, she was too preoccupied to muster much sympathy for anyone else right now.

"Yeah, I'm fine." She took a deep breath and stood, wobbling for only a second on the skates. This was not how she had imagined the bet going. When she cooked up the stupid idea, she had figured on having a few days to at least practice.

Well, not really. If she was honest with herself, she never even imagined that Alec would agree to it. But if he had, then she would have had a few days to practice.

So much for her imagination.

She took another deep breath then followed Ian from the locker room. It didn't take too long for her gait to even out and she muttered a thankful prayer. She only hoped that she didn't sprawl face-first as soon as she stepped on the ice.

Her right hand clenched around the stick, getting used to the feel of it, getting used to the fit of the bulky glove—which was too big to begin with. This would have been so much easier if all she had to do was put on a pair of skates. She had never considered the possibility of having to put all the gear on, right down to the helmet that was a heavy weight bearing down on her head.

She really needed to do something with her imagination and its lack of thinking things all the way through.

AJ took another deep breath when they finally reached the ice. She reached out to open the door but was stopped by Ian.

"Listen, AJ, I'm not even going to pretend I know what's going on or why you think you can do this, but I'll give you some advice. Shoot fast and low, and aim for the five and two holes—those are Alec's weak spots. The five hole is—"

"Between the legs, I know." AJ winced at the sharpness of her voice. Ian was only trying to help her. He had no reason to realize she knew anything about ice hockey, and not just because she liked to write about it. She offered him a smile to take the bite from her words then slammed the butt of the stick down against the door latch so it would swing open. Two steps later and she was standing on a solid sheet of thick ice.

AJ breathed deeply several times then slowly made her way to the other side of the rink, where Alec was nonchalantly leaning against the top post of the net talking to Nathan. They both watched as she skated up to them and came to a smooth stop. Alec's face was expressionless as he studied her, and she wondered what thoughts were going through his mind. Probably nothing she really wanted to know.

Nathan nodded at her, offering a small smile. She had to give the guy some credit for not laughing in her face when she asked his opinion on her idea. "Well, at least it looks like you've been on skates before. That's a plus."

AJ didn't say anything, just absently nodded in his direction. The carefree attitude she had been aiming for was destroyed by the helmet sliding down over her forehead. She pushed it back on her head then glanced at the five pucks lined neatly on the goal line. All she had to do was get one of them across. Just one.

She didn't have a chance.

She pushed the pessimistic thought to the back of her mind. "So, do I get a chance to warm up or take a practice shot?"

Alec sized her up then briskly shook his head. "No."

AJ swallowed and glanced at the pucks, then back at Alec. "Alrighty then. A man of few words. That's what I like about you, Kolchak." AJ though he might have cracked a smile behind his mask but she couldn't be sure. She sighed and leaned on her stick, trying to look casual and hoping it didn't slip out from under her and send her sprawling. "So, what are the rules?"

"Simple. You get five chances to shoot. If you score, you win. If you don't, I win." Alec swept the pucks to the side with the blade of his stick so Nathan could pick them up. She followed the moves with her eyes and tried to ignore the pounding in her chest.

She had so much riding on this. Something told her that Alec was dead serious about being left alone if she lost. It had been a stupid idea, and she wondered if she would have had better luck at trying to wear him down the old-fashioned way.

She studied his posture and decided probably not. He had been mostly patient with her up to this point, but even she knew he would have reached his limit soon.

"All or nothing, then. Fair enough. So, are you ready?"

AJ didn't hear his response but thought it was probably something sarcastic. She sighed then turned to follow Nathan to the center line, her heart beating too fast as her feet glided across the ice. She shrugged her shoulders, trying to readjust the bulk of the pads, and watched as Nathan lined the pucks up.

He finished then straightened and faced her, an unreadable expression on his face. He finally grinned and shook his head.

"I have no idea if you know what you're doing or not, but good luck. You're going to need it."

"Gee, thanks."

Nathan walked across the ice to the bench and leaned against the outer boards, joining a few of the other players gathered there. AJ wished they were gone, that they had something better to do than stand around and watch her make a fool of herself.

Well, she had brought it on herself.

She closed her eyes and inhaled deeply, pushing everything from her mind except what she was about to do. When she opened her eyes again, her gaze was on the first puck. Heavy, solid...nothing more than a slab of black rubber...

Okay, so she wasn't going to have any luck becoming one with the puck. Stupid idea. AJ had never understood that whole Zen thing anyway.

She swallowed and began skating in small circles, testing her ankles as she turned first one way then another, testing the stick as she swept it back and forth across the ice in front of her. Not too bad. Maybe she hadn't forgotten—

"Sometime today would be nice!"

AJ winced at the sarcasm in Alec's voice and wished she had some kind of comeback for him. Instead she mumbled to herself and got into position behind the first puck. She didn't even look up to see if he was ready. Didn't ask if it was okay to start, she just pushed off hard and skated, the stick out in front of her.

This was her one shot, she couldn't blow it.

PLAYING THE GAME
The York Bombers Book 1

Harland Day knows what it's like to be on rock bottom: he was there once before, years ago when his mother walked out and left him behind. But he learned how to play the game and survived, crawling his way up with the help of a friend-turned-lover. This time is different: he has nobody to blame but himself for his trip to the bottom. His mouth, his attitude, his crappy play that landed him back in the minors instead of playing pro hockey with the Baltimore Banners. And this time, he doesn't have anyone to help him out, not when his own selfishness killed the most important relationship he ever had.

Courtney Williams' life isn't glamorous or full of fame and fortune but she doesn't need those things to be happy. She of all people knows there are more important things in life. And, for the most part, she's been able to forget what could have been--until Harland gets reassigned to the York Bombers and shows back up in town, full of attitude designed to hide the man underneath. But the arrogant hockey player can't hide from her, the one person who knows him better than anyone else. They had been friends. They had been lovers. And then they had been torn apart by misunderstanding and betrayal.

But some ties are hard to break. Can they look past what had been and move forward to what could be? Or will the sins of the past haunt them even now, all these years later?

Turn the page for a preview of PLAYING THE GAME, the launch title of The York Bombers, now available.

The third drink was still in his hand, virtually untouched. He glanced down at it, briefly wondered if he should just put it down and walk away. It was still early, not even eleven yet. Maybe if he stuck it out for another hour; maybe if he finished this drink and let the whiskey loosen him up. Or maybe if he just paid attention to the girl draped along his side—

Maybe.

He swirled the glass in his hand and brought it to his mouth, taking a long sip of mostly melted ice. The girl next to him—what the fuck was her name?—pushed her body even closer, the swell of her barely-covered breast warm against the bare flesh of his arm.

"So you're a hockey player, right? One of Zach's teammates?"

Her breath held a hint of red wine, too sweet. Harland tried not to grimace, pushed the memories at bay as his stomach lurched. He tightened his grip on the glass—if he was too busy holding something, he couldn't put his arm around her or push her away—and glanced down. The girl looked like she was barely old enough to be in this place. A sliver of fright shot through him. They did card here, right? He wasn't about to be busted picking up someone underage, was he?

She had a killer body, slim and lean with just enough muscle tone in her arms and legs to reassure him that she didn't starve herself and probably worked out. Long tanned legs that went on for miles and dainty feet shoved into shoes that had to have heels at least five inches tall. He grimaced and briefly wondered how the hell she was even standing in them.

Of course, she *was* leaning against him, her full breasts pushing against his arm and chest. Maybe that was because she couldn't stand in those ridiculous heels. Heels like that weren't meant for walking—they were fuck-me heels, meant for the bedroom.

He looked closer, at her platinum-streaked hair carefully crafted in a fuck-me style and held in place by what had to be a full can of hairspray—or whatever the fuck women used nowadays. Thick mascara coated her lashes, or maybe they weren't even her real lashes, now that he was actually looking. No, he doubted they were real. That was a shame because from what he could see, she had pretty eyes, kind of a smoky gray set off by the shimmery eyeshadow coloring her lids. Hell, maybe those eyes weren't even real, maybe they were just colored contacts.

Fuck. Wasn't anything real anymore? Wasn't anyone who they really claimed to be? And why the fuck was he even worried about it when all he had to do was nod and smile and take her by the hand and lead her out? Something told him he wouldn't even have to bother with taking her home—or in his case, to a motel. No, he was pretty sure all he had to do was show her the backseat of his Expedition and that would be it.

Her full lips turned down into a pout and Harland realized she was waiting for him to answer. Yeah, she had asked him a question. What the hell had she asked?

Oh, yeah—

"Uh, yeah. Yeah, I play hockey." He took another sip of the watery drink and glanced around the crowded club. Several of his teammates were scattered around the bar, their faces alternately lit and shadowed by the colored lights pulsing in time to the music.

Jason pulled his tongue from some girl's throat long enough to motion to the mousy barmaid for a fresh drink. His gaze caught Harland's and a wide grin split his face when he nodded.

Harland got the message loud and clear. How could he miss it, when the nod was toward the girl hanging all over him? Jason was congratulating him on hooking up, encouraging him to take the next step.

Harland took another sip and looked away. Tension ran through him, as solid and real as the hand running along his chest. He looked down again, watched as slender fingers worked their way into his shirt. Nails scraped across the bare flesh of his chest, teasing him.

Annoying him.

He put the drink on the bar and reached for her hand, his fingers closing around her wrist to stop her. The girl looked up, a frown on her face. But she didn't move her hand away. No, she kept trying to reach for him instead.

"What'd you say your name was?"

"Does it matter?" Her lips tilted up into a seductive smile, full of heated promise as her fingers wiggled against his chest.

Did it matter? It shouldn't, not when all Harland had to do was smile back and release her hand and let her continue. Or take her hand and lead her outside. So why the fuck was he hesitating? Why didn't he do just that? That was why he came here, wasn't it? To let go. Loosen up. Hook up, get things out of his system.

No. That may be why Jason and Zach and the others were here and why they brought him along—but that wasn't why he was here. So yeah, her name mattered. Maybe not to him, not in that sense. He just wanted to know she was interested in *him* and not what he did. That he wasn't just a trophy for her, a conquest to be bragged about to her friends in the morning.

He gently tightened his hand around her wrist and pulled her arm away, out of reach of his chest. "Yeah. It matters."

Something flashed in her eyes—surprise? Impatience? Hell if he knew. He watched her struggle with a frown, almost like she didn't want him to see it. Then she pasted another bright smile on her face, this one a little too forced, and pulled her arm from his grasp.

"It's Shayla." She stepped even closer, running her hand along his chest and down, her finger tracing the waistband of his jeans.

He almost didn't stop her. Temptation seized him, fisting his gut, searing his blood. It would be easy, so easy.

Too easy.

Then a memory of warm brown eyes, wide with innocence, came to mind. Clear, sharp and almost painful. Harland closed his eyes, his breath hitching in his chest as the picture in his mind grew, encompassing soft brown hair and perfect lips, curled in a trembling smile.

"Fuck." His eyes shot open. He grabbed the girl's hand—Shayla's—just as she started to stroke him through the worn denim. Her own eyes narrowed and she made no attempt to hide her frown this time.

"What are you doing?" Her voice was sharp, biting.

"I could ask you the same thing."

Her hand twisted in his grip. Once, twice. "Zach told me you needed to loosen up. That you were looking for a little fun."

Zach had put her up to this? Harland should have

known. He narrowed his eyes, not surprised when the girl suddenly stiffened. Could she see his distaste. Sense his condemnation? He leaned forward, his mouth close to her ear, his voice flat and cold.

"Maybe you want me to whip my cock out right here so you can get on your knees and suck me off? Have everyone watch? Will that do it for you?"

She ripped her hand from his grasp and pushed him away, anger coloring her face. "You're a fucking asshole."

Harland straightened and fixed her with a flat smile. "You're right. I am."

She said something else, the words too low for him to hear, then spun around and walked away. Her steps were short, angry, and he had to bite back a smile when she teetered to the side and almost fell.

Loathing filled him, leaving him cold and empty. Not loathing of the girl—no, the loathing was all directed at himself. What the fuck was his problem?

The girl was right: he was a fucking asshole. A loathsome bastard.

Harland yanked the wallet from his back pocket and pulled out several bills, enough to cover whatever he'd had to drink and then some. He tossed down the watered whiskey, barely feeling the slight burn as it worked its way down his throat. Then he turned and stormed toward the door, ignoring the sound of his name being called.

He should have gone home, back to the three-bedroom condo he was now forced to share with the sorry excuse that passed for his father. But he wasn't in the mood to deal with his father's bullshit, not in the mood to deal with anything. So he drove, with no destination in mind, needing distance.

...om the spectacle he had just made of

...ce from what he had become.

...ance from who he was turning into.

...ut how in the hell was he supposed to distance ...elf...from himself?

Harland turned into a residential neighborhood, driving blindly, his mind on autopilot. He finally stopped, eased the SUV against the curb, and cut the engine.

Silence greeted him. Heavy, almost accusing. He rested his head against the steering wheel and squeezed his eyes shut. He didn't need to look around to know where he was, didn't need to view the quiet street filled with small houses that showed years of wear. Years of life and happiness and grief and torment.

"Fuck." The word came out in a strangled whisper and he straightened in the seat, running one hand down his face. Why did he keep coming here? Why did he keep tormenting himself?

She didn't want to see him, would probably shove him off the small porch if he ever dared to knock on the door. He knew that, as sure as he knew his own name.

As sure as he knew that she'd be sickened by what he had become. Three years had gone by. Three years where he'd never bothered to even contact her. Hell, maybe he was being generous. Maybe he was giving himself more importance than he deserved. Maybe she didn't even remember him.

He rubbed one hand across his eyes and took in a ragged breath, then turned his head to the side. The house was dark, just like almost every other house on the block. But he didn't need light to see it, not when it was so clear in his mind.

A simple cottage style home, with plain w. siding that was always one season away from needi a new coat of paint. Flowerbeds filled with explodin color that hid the age of the house. A small backyard filled with more flowers and a picnic table next to the old grill, where something was always being fixed during the warmer months.

An image of each room filled his mind, one after the other, like a choppy movie playing on an old screen. Middle class, blue collar—but full of laughter and warm memories. He knew the house, better than his own.

He should. He'd spent more time here growing up than he had at his own run-down house the next street over. He had come here to escape, stayed because it was an oasis in his own personal desert of despair.

Until he had ruined even that.

He closed his eyes against the memories, shutting them out with a small whimper of pain. Then he started the truck and pulled away, trying to put distance between himself and the past.

A past that was suddenly more real than the present.

64600090R00161

Made in the USA
Middletown, DE
29 August 2019